The Water Babies

Retold by Josephine Poole
Illustrated by Jan Ormerod

The Millbrook Press
Brookfield, Connecticut

The Water Babies by Charles Kingsley was first published in 1863

This retelling first published in the United States in 1998 by
The Millbrook Press, Inc.
2 Old New Milford Road
Brookfield, Connecticut 06804

First published in Great Britain in 1996 by
Macdonald Young Books, an imprint of
Wayland Publishers Limited
61 Western Road
Hove, East Sussex BN3 1JD

Text © 1996 Josephine Poole
Illustrations © 1996 Jan Ormerod

Designed by Small House Design
Printed in Hong Kong by Dah Hua

Library of Congress Cataloging-in-Publication Data

Poole, Josephine.
    The water babies/Charles Kingsley; retold by Josephine Poole;
illustrated by Jan Ormerod.
        p.   cm.
    Summary: The adventures of Tom, a sooty little chimney sweep
with a great longing to be clean, who is stolen by fairies and turned
into a water baby.
    ISBN 0-7613-0411-8 (lib. bdg.)
    [1. Fairy tales. 2. Chimney sweeps—Fiction.] I. Kingsley,
Charles, 1819-1875. Water-babies. II. Ormerod, Jan, ill.
III. Title.
PZ8.P8Wat   1998
[Fic]—dc21   97-31894
                                                 CIP
                                                 AC

The Water Babies

Retold by Josephine Poole
Illustrated by Jan Ormerod

The Millbrook Press
Brookfield, Connecticut

Chapter One

Once there was a boy called Tom, and he had no mother or father. He lived long ago, when England was greener and wilder than it is now. But English cities were very black and dirty, and the poor people who lived in them were very poor indeed.

Tom worked for a man called Grimes, who was a master sweep. All the houses in those days had coal fires, and fires make smoke and soot, so there was plenty for Tom to do, cleaning the chimneys. Grimes took all the money he earned and spent it on clothes for himself, and gambling, and beer in the pub. But little Tom was as poor as any child could be.

He had never learned to read or write. He never washed, because there was no water where he lived—not that he cared about that! He didn't like climbing into the black chimneys, grazing his elbows and knees, and getting soot in his eyes. He cried when Grimes beat him, which he often did, or when he was hungry. But he still had time to play leapfrog and tag with the other boys, and chuck stones at the legs of the carriage horses as they trotted past, which he thought good fun, as long as there was somewhere to hide. He was cheerful and bold, and he dreamed of the good times coming, when he would be a master sweep like Grimes, and sit drinking and smoking in the pub, and play cards for money. He would have boys to work for him then, and knock them about the way Grimes did. He would make them carry home the soot sacks, while he rode in front on a donkey, with a dog at his heels and a flower in his buttonhole. Hooray! He'd look like a king—a king at the head of his army!

One day a smart little pony trotted into the alley where Tom lived, with a smart little groom on his back. Tom was just creeping behind a wall with half a brick ready to throw, when the groom spotted him and called out to know where he could find Mr. Grimes.

Tom came out then and took orders. Mr. Grimes was to go to Sir John Harthover's, at Harthover Place, the next morning, because the regular sweep had been sent to prison, and the chimneys needed cleaning. Then the groom rode away before Tom had a chance to ask what the sweep had gone to prison for. And he looked so neat and clean, with his brown gaiters, brown jacket and breeches, and white tie with a pin in it, that Tom longed to throw the brick at him. But he didn't.

Now Harthover Place was a grand house, one of the finest in the north country, and when Tom told Grimes that they had been asked there to sweep chimneys, he was so pleased that he knocked Tom down and went straight off to the pub. On the next morning they got up at three o'clock, and Grimes knocked Tom down again, partly because his head hurt from drinking too much, and partly to show him how important it was to do a good job. But Tom would have done his best anyway. He had heard people talk about Harthover Place, and although he had never been there, he was sure it must be the most wonderful house in the world.

It was a long way from the city. Grimes rode the donkey in front, and Tom walked behind, carrying the bundle of brushes. They went out of the alley and up the street, past the rows of houses with closed shutters and the tired policemen. They walked through the village where the miners lived who worked in the coal pit, but they were still asleep. Then they came out into open country and plodded along the black, dusty road between walls made of black slag, which is coal not fit for burning. The only sound was the groan and thump of the pit engine in the next field. After a while Tom stopped to look back at the city, but all he could see of it were the roofs shining gray in the gray dawn.

Soon the road turned white, and the walls were made of pale stone, with grass and bright flowers growing against them, and the groaning of the engine died away in the distance. Now the first lark began singing, but it was so high up that although Tom looked and looked, he couldn't see any bird in the clear blue sky. Otherwise, all was silent, except for the clip-clop of the patient donkey, and Tom's small bare feet pattering along the road.

How beautiful everything looked so early in the morning! A light covering of mist lay over the sloping green meadows, as if the earth was still asleep under a blanket. Tom had never been so far into the country before, and he longed to drop the sooty brushes and climb over a gate and pick buttercups, and shout to startle the cows dozing under the huge elm trees, and hunt for birds' nests in the bushes along the stream. But Grimes rode on without a pause, with never a glance to right or left, and Tom had to trot to keep up with him.

By and by they met a poor Irishwoman, who was trudging along with a bundle on her back. She wore a gray shawl over her head, and a crimson flannel petticoat, but she had no shoes or stockings on, and she limped as if her feet hurt. All the same she was a tall, handsome woman, with bright gray eyes and thick black hair. Grimes liked the look of her, and he called out, "This is rough going for pretty feet! You can ride behind me if you like."

"No, thank you," she said quietly. "I shall walk behind with your boy."

"Please yourself," growled Grimes, and stuck his pipe back in his mouth.

So the Irishwoman walked with Tom and asked him all about himself, till he thought he had never met such a pleasant lady. He asked her where she lived.

"Oh, I come from far, far away. I live by the sea," she said.

"The sea! What's that?" He knew it was water, but that was all he knew. He had never seen the sea. So she told him how it roared when it was stormy, and dashed itself on the rocks in clouds of spray, and how it could break up a great ship as if it was made of straw. But then, she said, on calm summer days it lay so quiet, so still, that children could bathe and play in it. It sounded like such an enchanted place to Tom, he wished with all his heart to go there himself.

Now the road led downhill, and at the bottom there was a shallow cave under a crag. A spring of water bubbled up inside it as clear as glass, and ran away under the road in a swift stream. Here they stopped, and Tom stared at the cave and wondered what could live inside, and whether it flew out at night. Then he began picking the flowers that grew near, blue and golden and white, and the Irishwoman helped him, and showed him how to tie them into a bunch with a tough stem of grass. But Grimes got off his donkey and knelt down by the spring and plunged his ugly head into it. He did this again and again, until the water was exceedingly dirty.

Tom cried out in astonishment, "Why, master, that's the first time I've ever seen you wash!"

"Wash!" exclaimed Grimes in disgust, shaking his head to get the water out of his ears. "What would a master sweep like me want with washing! I'm too hot, that's all."

"But I want a wash," whined poor Tom. "It's nicer than our town pump, and there is no policeman here to drive me away."

"Shut your mouth," snarled Grimes. "Keep out of it! Did you sit up drinking half the night? Is your head aching fit to burst? No! Clear off!"

But Tom stuck out his tongue at him and ran down to the stream, and began to wash his dirty hands and arms, and his sooty face.

Now Grimes was still angry because the woman had chosen Tom instead of him for company, so he swore at him and grabbed him and started to beat him. But Tom was used to that, and kicked him on the shins as hard as he could.

"Aren't you ashamed of yourself, Thomas Grimes?" cried the Irishwoman.

Grimes looked up. He was startled because she knew his name, but he only said, "No, and I never have been," and went on beating Tom.

"That's true!" she said. "If there was any shame in you, you'd have gone to Vendale, long ago."

"Vendale? What's that about Vendale?" shouted Grimes. He stopped beating Tom and turned on the woman. Tom was afraid he would hit her, but she looked at him so fiercely that he cursed her instead. "Who are you?" he said.

"Never mind who I am. I know all about you, and you'd better leave that boy alone, or I'll tell what I know."

Grimes went back to his donkey without a word.

"Stop!" said the Irishwoman. "I have something else to say to you both before we meet again, which we will do, you can be sure of that. Those who wish to be clean, clean they will be; and those who wish to be foul, foul they will be. Remember!"

She turned away into the meadow. Grimes stood thunderstruck a moment, and then he rushed after her, shouting, "You come back!" But she had gone.

Where was she? There was nowhere to hide. Grimes and Tom stared in all directions. There was no sign of her, nothing at all, not so much as a footprint in the dewy grass. She had—vanished.

Grimes was frightened then. He filled up his little pipe in silence and got back on his donkey, and he left Tom in peace.

Chapter Two

Tom and Grimes went on until at last they reached the massive wrought-iron gates of Harthover Place. Tom looked between the bars, down a long, long avenue of lime trees stretching across a great park, as far as his eyes could see. He was wondering what could live in the park, when he noticed antlers sticking up through the bracken, where the deer were lying asleep. Then he was scared because he believed that deer ate children, but Grimes had rung the bell at the lodge, and now the keeper came out and unlocked the gates. So Tom took up his bundle of brushes and walked bravely through, but he was glad when the keeper said he would come with them to the house. The keeper was in charge of all the game in the park, and he had heard about Grimes. He guessed he would take any chance to steal a pheasant or two, to hide at the bottom of the soot bag.

They set off together down the avenue. Tom had never seen such enormous trees. They lifted their green and golden leaves up, up to the sky itself, which looked as if it was resting on top. But a strange humming noise came from all about the branches, which followed them as they walked. It puzzled him so much, that at last he plucked up courage to ask what it was.

"That?" said the keeper. "That's the bees in the lime flowers."

"Please, sir, what are bees?"

"Bees make honey."

"Please, sir, what is honey?"

"Shut up," growled Grimes.

"Leave him alone," said the keeper. "He's a polite little chap, which he won't be for long if he stays with you."

Grimes laughed, as if that was a compliment.

"I wish I lived in a place like this," said Tom. "I wish I was a gamekeeper, and wore green cords, and had a real dog whistle hanging from my button like you."

The keeper pinched his ear, but kindly, and went on talking to Grimes in a low voice. Now Tom could see a second pair of iron gates at the bottom of the avenue. Behind them towered the tall gray stone and red brick chimneys of Sir John Harthover's Place.

What an enormous palace of a house it was! Tom walked with his mouth open in astonishment and his eyes round with surprise, wondering when such a marvelous place was built, and whether one man had built it, and who that person was, and how much it had cost. He hoped the keeper would lead them up the wide stone stairs, and blow his whistle for someone to open the huge front door. But alas, when they reached the gates, they didn't go through them. They had to go all the way around to the back, and it was a long way around.

They entered the house by a door that needed painting, and were presently met by a lady wearing a flowered dressing gown, who was so exceedingly smart, and so fearfully proud, that Tom thought she must be Sir John's wife. They stood in the passage while she gave Grimes very exact instructions, and he jabbed Tom with his elbow and muttered, "You'll remember that, you little beggar," and Tom tried to take in what was being said. Then the lady, who was really the housekeeper, showed them into a very splendid room, but all the furniture and pictures and ornaments had been huddled together under cloths and brown paper. Here she left them with a haughty housemaid, who stayed to make sure that Grimes didn't steal anything.

And now came the moment that Tom dreaded, for with a shove and a kick he had to climb into the grate and creep up the black sooty chimney, and it was dark, pitch dark inside. Only a small square of light far below marked the room where Grimes waited, and very soon there was no light at all. Tom climbed up and up, sweeping as he went.

Soon the chimney divided, and he crawled to the right, following his nose which he couldn't see in the dark. Soon it divided again, so he turned left, always sweeping, sweeping—and the soft black soot covered him completely so that he looked like a black monkey. He was expecting a little light from the chimney pots that were open to the sky. But no matter how he climbed, there wasn't so much as a glimmer.

Tom was used to the town chimneys, which were tall and narrow and not complicated. But Harthover Place was so very old, and had been altered so many times, and its chimneys twisted and divided so often that he was completely bewildered. He knew he was lost, but he didn't worry any more than a mole underground. He'd find his way out in the end, and sure enough, at last he saw light below him, and shinned down, expecting to see Grimes and the housemaid and the familiar room. Instead, when his feet touched the bars of the grate, and he peeped out from the fireplace, he found himself somewhere quite different—quite different from anything he had ever seen.

When people wanted their chimneys swept, they always rolled up the carpets, took down the curtains, and covered everything against the soot. So Tom had never seen such a room, and he stepped out onto the hearth rug and stared all around, and was amazed because it all looked so pretty.

The carpet was white with a pink flowery pattern. The furniture was all white, and pictures in gold frames hung on the white walls. The white curtains drawn across the window glowed in the early morning sunshine. Someone must be still asleep in here, and then Tom saw who it was.

A little girl lay in the white bed, with her golden hair spread over the pillow. She was the most beautiful child he had ever seen, and he gazed at her and wondered if she could be really alive, or whether she was a wax doll such as they sold in shops. He was just going to creep up to the bed to look at her properly, when he caught sight of something very ugly in the spotless room.

There was a small black hideous person standing near him, all covered in soot from its rough hair to its toes. It had ragged clothes and grinning teeth. What could such a monster be doing here! Tom was about to dash at it and drive it out, when—alas, poor Tom!—he understood that the monster was himself. There he stood, reflected in a mirror. He had never seen the whole of himself before.

He burst into tears of rage and shame. He tried to scramble back into the

chimney, but in his haste he knocked over the poker, and it made such a clatter in the grate that the little girl woke up. When she saw black Tom crouching there, she gave a piercing scream, and a fat old nurse ran in, still wearing her nightcap. She rushed at Tom and grabbed at his jacket, but he wriggled free and was across the room and out of the window in a moment.

A tree grew just outside, which was lucky for him. He leapt for a branch and climbed down like a cat, raced across the lawn and squeezed between the garden railings. He was running across the park toward the woods while the old nurse still stood at the window, shrieking, "Fire! Thieves! Murder!"

A gardener heard the noise, looked around, and saw Tom escaping. He dropped his scythe and cut himself on the leg, but he followed, waving his arms and shouting. The screams frightened the dairymaid so much that she upset all the cream, but she left it for the cats and ran after Tom. The groom rushed out of the stable and never thought of shutting the door, he was so eager to catch him. In the field behind the house, the haymakers one and all gave chase, waving rakes and forks, while the horses ambling homeward upset the wagon in the hedge. The keeper in the green cords was setting a trap. When everyone dashed past him shouting, "Fire! Murder! Thieves!" he jumped up and spiked his finger with it, but that didn't stop him from running after Tom. Grimes was carrying a soot sack into the yard. He heard the commotion and dropped it all over the gravel, but he ran out, cursing Tom. And last of all, old Sir John opened his study window and looked up at the nurse, and a swallow dropped a blob in his eye so that later on he had to call the doctor, but he ran out of the house and joined in the chase. Everyone was running, even the Irishwoman. She had come up to the house to beg, but she threw away her bundle and ran with the others. But Tom ran faster than any of them.

He made for the woods, and in he dived, headfirst among the bushes. Oh, what a horrible surprise! Nobody came in here but rabbits and pheasants. The bushes caught him and tried to wrench off his clothes. The ground was covered with brambles, which wound around his ankles and ran thorns into

his feet. It was nearly as dark as a chimney, and far more painful—he was scratched, and poked, and switched all over.

Although he had done nothing wrong, the noise made him very afraid of being caught. The shouts of his pursuers were getting louder and louder. He was going to be caught like a rat in a trap, and his sooty face was streaked with tears as well as sweat, when suddenly, in his blind scramble, he came head-on against a wall.

The wall hit him between the eyes, but he didn't care. He guessed at once that it marked the boundary of the woods, and he was up and over it like a squirrel. And now he was out on the moor, which is called Harthover Fell, and nothing but sheep grass, and rocks, and heather stretching away in front of him as far as he could see.

Tom was cunning, and he didn't run on across the moor, where anyone could have spotted him from the woods. Instead, he doubled back, and trotted along under the wall for half a mile, until he heard the shouts dying away in the distance.

But the Irishwoman saw which way Tom went. She had followed him across the park and into the woods, and she climbed the wall after him. It was very strange, because he did look around from time to time, and yet he never saw her behind him.

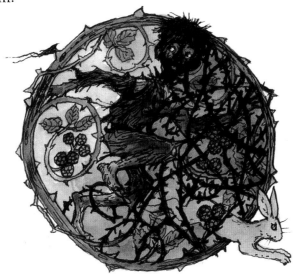

Chapter Three

Now Tom was right out in the heather. It was rough going, but he jogged on steadily, while he looked about him at this unknown world, where the wild creatures were at home and he was the stranger. There were lizards sunning themselves on the rocks. Tom was afraid they were snakes, but they were more timid than he was. Then he came upon a large, brown vixen rolling about on her back in the sunshine, with her four cubs jumping over her and snatching at her legs, and trying to pull her along by the tail. As soon as she saw Tom, she jumped up and caught one of them in her mouth, and they all slipped away between the rocks.

So Tom went on. As he was plodding up a sandy rise, he had a terrible fright, because something seemed to explode in his face. But he had only startled an old cock grouse, who shirred up like a firecracker—"Cur-ru-u-uck-cock-kick-kick"—and sped home to warn his family that the world was certainly coming to an end.

The moor changed as Tom trudged on. There was more rock and less heather. The sun was gradually moving up the sky, and the slabs of limestone were hot as well as rough to walk on. He had to jump the cracks between them, and sometimes he slipped and bruised himself. But he liked this great wild place, whose only boundary was the cloudless sky. So he climbed over the rocks, and toiled bravely across the burning slabs and through the dry, prickly heather, and he never thought of turning back. What was there to turn back for?

And all the time the Irishwoman was following behind him. If he had seen her, he might have stopped to talk and been glad of her company. But he never saw her at all.

It was so hot now that the air seemed to dance all around him. Poor Tom stumbled often as he walked, and often tripped and hurt his toes. He longed for a drink. He listened by a hole in the rock, because he fancied he could hear water tinkling deep down at the bottom of it. But though he was as brave as any sweep could be, he didn't dare to climb down such a chimney.

The heat made him giddy, and sometimes he heard bells ringing. "Bells! That means a church," he told himself. "A church means people. Someone will give me a bite to eat and a drink." So he went on, encouraged, believing those were real bells he heard, though in fact they were ringing inside his head.

Now he had come to the very top of the moor. He stopped and looked around. He was amazed that he had walked so far and climbed so high. Behind him lay Harthover, far away below—there were the very chimneys where he had lost himself, and the garden and the park and the dark wood. Looking to the left, he could see smoke hanging over the city where he lived, and beyond, the shining river. He could see how it gradually widened until it met the sea, which lay like a piece fallen out of the sky, it was so calm and blue. In front of him the country spread out like a map following the gentle slopes of the hills. There were tiny villages and farms down there, fields speckled with cows, corn fields, and hay, all divided into patterns by the darker green lines of the hedges. And on his right the moor stretched up and up, shimmering blue and more blue, until it seemed to dissolve into the sky.

But just below him, he saw something that made his poor tired heart beat faster. A deep, green valley lay at his feet, with a stream glinting between the trees. There was a gray roof with a tall chimney close to the stream, and a little garden set out with flowers and vegetables. He spotted a woman in the garden, no bigger than a fly, directly beneath him so he fancied he could have dropped a pebble onto her bonnet. Even from up here he could tell that she was a good sort. He'd drink at the stream, and then he'd go to her for something to eat. Why, he could be down there in a couple of minutes!

That was what he thought, and he began clambering down, though it was fearfully steep, and he was very tired indeed.

And he never saw the Irishwoman coming down behind him.

Chapter Four

Tom was looking into Vendale from the top of Lewthwaite Crag. Even a fox would have chosen a different way down to the beautiful little valley where he longed to be, but he was desperate and much too tired to think clearly. He only knew that there was water, and he had to get to it.

His first obstacle was a steep, heathery slope. The heather hid a scattering of crumbly brown stones, which were very painful to his feet, and often rolled away under him, so he sat down with a bump. It hurt a good deal, but he kept going. After a while, the heather ran out, and he found himself on a sloping ledge of short springy grass, where tiny flowers and herbs grew. He crept to the edge, and peered over.

He saw that he was at the top of a series of enormous steps. He let himself down to the next, and the next. Then he arrived on a ledge much steeper than the others, as steep as the roof of a house, where he didn't dare to stand but slid down on his bottom. That ledge ended in a sheer drop. He would have been stuck then, except that he found a crack, and crawled down inside it, holding himself with his elbows and knees, the way he would in a chimney. He got across the next ledge, and there was another great drop, the same or worse, and he had to find another crack to get down by. And so it went on, until he was trembling all over with the strain, and yet, when he looked down at the glittering stream, it seemed so close that he still believed his troubles were nearly over.

At the bottom of that terrible staircase, there was a rough bank where trees and bushes grew thickly among the rocks. It was shady, but it was so warm and damp under the leaves that he could hardly breathe. The bells were ringing so loudly now in his ears, he never doubted that there was a church further on.

He looked down on the stream and could even see the pebbles at the bottom. He told himself that in just a few minutes he'd be plunging in his face for a drink.

Now he was out of the trees, but the struggle was not over yet. In front of him lay a tumble of rocks that had fallen off the face of the crag. They were all shapes and sizes—some as small as his head, others bigger than a stagecoach. He had to crawl and jump and slide and scramble over them, and it took him a long time, though he thought he was hurrying. He was sweating so much that the soot ran off him in a trail of black smears.

And so, in the end, he found himself in the valley. Now there was only one little field between him and the cottage. He stumbled on—all he knew was that he needed help, and he had seen the woman in the garden.

The cottage was small and very neat. The door was open, and an odd noise droned through. He didn't wonder what it could be. He tottered up to the threshold and stopped there under the roses and honeysuckle that grew around the doorway.

He had come to Vendale school. Several children paused in the middle of repeating their lesson, and stared at his filthy, tattered figure. The smallest began to cry, while some big boys burst out laughing and made faces. The old cat got up and arched his back and hissed at Tom, and the cuckoo shot out of the clock and shouted eleven times, not at him personally, but marking the hour of the day. So at last the old lady who kept the school got an idea that something unusual was happening, and she looked around and saw him. She had changed her gardening bonnet for a white cap tied severely under her chin.

"What are you doing here?" she exclaimed. "You're a chimney sweep—get along with you this instant! I won't have sweeps here."

"Water," whispered Tom.

"Water? There's plenty in the stream," she told him sharply.

"I can't get there." Poor Tom collapsed on the step and leaned his aching head against the door.

Now the old lady was really very kind, but she had her own reasons for hating all chimney sweeps. She put on her spectacles and looked at him properly. Presently she said, "I do believe you're poorly, and you're only a child after all, even if you are a sweep." She went away into the next room, and came back with a cup of milk and some bread. "Here you are," she said, bending over him. "This will do you more good than water."

He gulped down the milk, and felt stronger.

"Where are you from?"

"Up there." He pointed back toward the sky.

"You're not telling me you've come down over Lewthwaite Crag? How did you get up there?"

"Over the moor from Harthover." He was too tired to think up a story. It didn't take long to tell her how it all happened.

"And you haven't stolen anything?"

"No."

"Poor little chap! All the way from the Place, and down over the crag! God must have guided you in your innocence. Come along, eat your bread!"

"I don't want it."

"It's good bread, I made it myself."

"I can't eat it." He raised his head and looked at her. "Is it Sunday?"

"No."

"But the church bells keep ringing—all the bells. It must be Sunday."

"You've a touch of the sun, that's the trouble. Come with me, I'll find you somewhere to lie down—I'd put you in my own bed if you weren't so dirty."

Tom tried to follow her, but he was so weak and giddy that he couldn't stand. The old lady put her arm around him, and helped him to a shed where she made him a bed of clean, sweet hay, and covered him with a rug. Then she went back to the cottage. She thought he would be safe there until school was over, at midday. She was sure he would go straight to sleep.

But he didn't.

His bed was soft, but he couldn't rest. He was too hot under the rug, but if he threw it off he started to shiver. He ached all over. He shut his eyes and thought he saw the little girl in her white bed. She sat up and exclaimed, "Oh, how dirty you are! Don't you ever wash?" Then he thought he heard the Irishwoman saying, "Those who wish to be clean, clean they will be," over and over again. Sometimes the words were so loud that they rang in his ears like the church bells, and sometimes they were so soft, he could scarcely hear them.

But soon the church bells came back and drowned everything. Oh, he was sure it must be Sunday! He wondered what a church was like—he had never

been inside one. He had an idea that if he could only find the church, the Irishwoman and the little girl would be there waiting for him. So he must wash—he must! He wouldn't be allowed into a church as he was, all covered with soot. He must go to the stream and wash.

Then he was standing in the middle of the meadow, though he couldn't at all remember how he got there. But he knew it was real and not a dream because he could feel the long grass tickling his legs, and the sun beat down on him so that he seemed to be on fire. He could see the stream and hear it, too, for it wasn't far away. He stumbled toward it and gazed down into the clear, cold water. The pebbles were shining at the bottom of it, and there were tiny silver fish which darted away when they saw his face.

He began to pull off his clothes, tearing them because he was in such a hurry—they were rags anyway. He sat down on the edge of the stream and put his poor sore feet into the water, and oh, it was such a lovely, cool feeling! He put in his legs while the bells rang louder and louder in his head. He muttered aloud, "I must be quick and clean myself, because they'll shut the door when the bells stop, and then I won't be able to get into the church." So he went down into the streaming water, and it felt to him like kind, healing hands that took all his pain away. So he slipped down, and down, until it covered him completely.

And the extraordinary thing was that the Irishwoman was there all the time, and yet he never saw her.

When she came to the stream she stepped straight into the water. Her shawl and her crimson petticoat floated away, and instead she was dressed in green water weed, with white water lilies in her hair. And the fairies who lived in that stream came and caught her in their arms and carried her away with them, because she was their queen.

"I have brought you a little brother," she told them. "But you mustn't let him see you, you mustn't speak to him, or play with him yet. There are many things he has to learn, and he will learn them from the other water creatures. You must look after him and make sure he doesn't get hurt."

The fairies were disappointed, because they would have liked to play with Tom. But they promised to make themselves invisible to him and to take good care of him. Then the Irishwoman who was their queen floated away down the stream, and down the river, and on—who knows where?

But little Tom lay in the stream, for he had fallen into the most restful, beautiful sleep that he had ever known. He dreamed about the green fields and the trees and the peaceful cows he had seen early that morning. And after a while he didn't dream at all.

Chapter Five

At midday the school closed and the children went home, and the old lady toddled off to the shed to see how Tom was. She expected to find him lying there fast asleep—but he had gone. She shaded her eyes and looked all around. She put on her spectacles, but there was no sign of him. Then she felt cross, thinking he had tricked her, the little vagabond sweep.

By this time Sir John and the gardener and the keeper and Grimes, and all the other people who had been hunting Tom, had given up and gone back to Harthover Place.

The first thing Sir John did was to call for the nurse, and talk to his daughter, whose name was Ellie. She was the little girl with golden hair.

"It was only a dirty little boy," said Ellie. "He looked like a goblin, but he didn't do any harm. He was crying and trying to get up the chimney."

Nothing had been stolen. Now Sir John was afraid that he had made a dreadful mistake.

He told Grimes he would give him twenty pounds if he brought Tom to Harthover, so that he could put things right. But Tom didn't come home, so the next day Grimes went back sulkily to Harthover Place. Sir John had already gone out, and he had to wait for him in the servants' hall, drinking strong beer to cheer himself up.

Good Sir John had had a sleepless night. He said to his wife, "My dear, I am very worried about that boy. He must have tried to cross the moor and got lost. I shall have to see if I can find him."

So he got up at five, and dressed, and mounted his pony. Five huntsmen went with him, with a bloodhound on a lead. This dog was huge, with a deep hollow voice like a bell. They led him as far as the wood, when they let him go, and he guided them to the place where Tom had climbed over the wall. Here he threw back his great head and bayed.

They broke down the wall enough to get through with the ponies, and the dog took them slowly across the moor. He was following yesterday's scent, and it was very faint in that dry weather. But that was why clever old Sir John had started out so early in the morning.

At last they came to the top of Lewthwaite Crag, and looked down into Vendale. And the dog bayed again, to say, "This is the way he went!"

They couldn't believe that Tom would have dared to climb down there. But they knew that the dog spoke the truth.

"God forgive us!" exclaimed Sir John. "Who will go down in case the boy is lying helpless somewhere? Oh, if I were only twenty years younger, I would go myself!" Then he slapped his pocket with his big red hand. "Fifty pounds to the man who brings him to me!"

Now the youngest groom had galloped after the search party. He was the same boy who had met Tom in the alley and given him the message for Grimes.

"I'll go, and never mind the money," he said. "I'll do it for the boy's sake. If he should be hiding somewhere, he won't be afraid of me."

So he gave them his pony to lead, and down he went. It took him a long time. He tore his clothes and burst his boots and braces; worst of all, he lost his gold tiepin with a horse on it, which he had won in a raffle. But he never saw a sign of Tom.

Meanwhile Sir John and the others rode all the way around to Vendale. The schoolchildren ran out and stroked the dog and the ponies. The old lady curtsied to Sir John.

"God bless you, Harthover," she said. "Welcome to Vendale—but what makes you sad on such a beautiful day?"

"We're looking for a child, dame, a sweep's poor boy that has run away."

"Oh Harthover!" she cried. "I believe I have seen that very boy—but he said he had done nothing wrong!"

"He was driven from the house by mistake. The hound here followed him all the way to the top of the crag. God knows. . . ."

The old lady began to weep. "Poor child! Poor little dear!" And she told them all she knew.

Then Sir John looked very grim. The dog was taken to the shed where the rug was still lying on the hay, and he bayed once. He led them over the track and on across the field to the stream. There were Tom's sooty rags all higgledy piggledy as he had torn them off. They searched the pockets and found three marbles, and a brass button on a string. They hunted along the bank, and at last they noticed a small black shape under the streaming water. This was what they were dreading, for they were sure it was Tom's body lying there drowned. They were wrong—they were absolutely wrong—but they believed he was dead.

They rode sorrowfully back to Harthover, and poor Ellie cried bitterly when she heard what had happened. In fact, Grimes was the only person who did not mourn for Tom, because Sir John gave him ten pounds, and he spent it all on drink.

Tom's remains were carefully lifted out and buried in the churchyard at Vendale, and the old lady kept fresh flowers on that small grave as long as she lived. But what they buried was no more Tom than an eggshell is a chicken. When a chicken hatches, it leaves its shell behind, and in the same way, Tom had left the shell of his chimney sweep life.

How had he done this? The answer was simple. While he was lying asleep in the stream, the fairies had come and transformed him, carefully and gently, into a water baby.

Chapter Six

Tom was now about as big as a minnow—just the right size to feel comfortable in the stream. He woke up swimming as easily as if he had been born in the water—which was true, in a way. He was spotlessly clean, as clean as the pebbles glinting at the bottom, and he had been cleaned inside as well, because he had no memory of his earthly existence. All those miserable times when he'd been hungry and tired and beaten, all those black chimneys, and black Grimes too being angry or drunk—Tom couldn't remember any of this. He couldn't even remember Harthover Place and the little girl with golden hair. His life had started all over again, and at first he was perfectly happy, with nothing to do but explore this underwater world.

There was plenty for him to eat among the plants that grew in the stream. He chewed the leaves and the cool green stems, and gobbled up the seeds. The water fairies kept him away from anything that might be poisonous, but they never let him see them.

He was so tiny now that he could swim after the freshwater shrimps who scuttled about in the gravel, the way rabbits do on land. Then he might find a quiet place where he could watch the caddises munching up twigs, as if they were candy, and building their houses around themselves from scraps of all sorts stuck together with glue. If he came to a deep, still pool, there grew the water forests—common plants that a person walking past would hardly notice, but which, now that Tom was so small, stretched up high above him with their long, green, gently swaying branches, where all kinds of tiny creatures climbed and swung and leapt.

Now Tom could talk to all these different creatures, and he might have had many friends. Unfortunately, he would poke them and tease and torment them, until they hid when they saw him and didn't come out again until he had gone. The water fairies pitied him, and longed to teach him how to behave, and play with him themselves. But they kept their promise, and poor Tom began to feel rather miserable, all on his own.

At last he went up to a caddis to ask her to come out and talk to him, but the door of her little stick and glue house was shut. So he unpicked it to see what she was doing inside, and found that she had grown a beak and tied up her whole head in a covering of pink skin. She couldn't say anything, but all her caddis friends put their heads out and started shrieking together, "Oh, you beastly boy! Why can't you leave us alone? She had just gone to sleep, and after a fortnight she would have woken up with such lovely wings, and been able to fly and lay eggs, and now you have broken in and she will die. Oh, it's too bad! Go away, you nasty, rough creature!"

Tom was sorry, but he didn't say so. He swam away to a pool of little trout. They scattered when they saw him, and he tried to catch them, but he was too clumsy. While he was chasing them, he blundered close to an alder root, where the water was very dark and still. Suddenly, out dashed an enormous old brown trout, ten times his own size, and gave him such a bump that he was winded and dizzy with fright!

So he went on in a very bad temper. Presently he noticed a hideous creature crouching under the bank. It was half as big as Tom, with six legs, and a fat paunch, and a great ugly head with two large eyes in its donkey face.

"Yah, boo!" jeered Tom. "I'm glad I don't look like you!" He waggled his tongue at it and made hideous faces, and was as rude as he could be—when suddenly—ouch!—a long arm with pincers shot out and snapped him by the nose!

"Yah, boo! Whad are you doing? Led go!"

"Leave me alone then," said the creature. "I want to split."

"I will, I probise," spluttered Tom. "Bud whad do you wad to splid for?"

"All my brothers and sisters have done it," said the creature, letting go of him. "They have spread out their wings and flown away, and I must split, I will split, I am absolutely determined to split!"

His last words came out in a shriek, as he swelled, and puffed, and stretched —and then—bingo! He began opening all down his back, and up to the top of his head.

And from the ugly shell emerged a slender, elegant creature, soft and smooth like Tom but as weak and wobbly as a child who has been ill for a long time. He began creeping slowly up a grass stem toward the surface of the water. He came out into the sunshine.

And as the sun warmed him and dried him, he began to change. His body strengthened and hardened, and developed the most brilliant colors—blue and yellow and black. Four large brown wings that had been lying on his back like crumpled tissue paper gradually unfolded and uncreased, and his great eyes sparkled like jewels.

"Oh, how beautiful you are!" cried Tom. He stretched out his arms, but the dragonfly whirred up from his grasp and hovered just out of reach.

"You can't catch me," he said. "I am the king of all the flies and lord of the river air! I shall feast on gnats, and marry a princess as beautiful as myself, and we will dance together in the sunshine!"

"Oh, don't go away!" said Tom. "Please don't! I want you for my friend!"

"All right," said the dragonfly. "But I must find something to eat first and have a look around. Gracious! What an enormous tree!"

It was only a dock, but the dragonfly was very nearsighted, and after the little water plants he was used to, it did look like a tree. He flew away, but he came back and told Tom about all the strange and wonderful things he had seen. So they were friends, and from that day Tom stopped teasing the water creatures. He had learned that the ugliest of them could turn into the most beautiful, and he even stopped chasing the trout. He caught flies for them instead (which was bad luck for the flies), and the trout tried to teach him how to somersault over the water the way they did when they felt a shower coming, but he could never manage it.

Soon after this, he had an alarming adventure.

Chapter Seven

Tom was sitting with the dragonfly on a lily leaf, listening to stories of his past life underwater and the strange things he had seen since in the world of earth and air. He was watching the gnats dance as he listened—they were quite safe, because the dragonfly had just eaten supper—and asking questions from time to time. He particularly liked to hear about the earth, because in some strange way he seemed to have a memory of it.

All at once he heard an extraordinary noise, like a pigeon, a puppy, a piglet, and some guinea pigs all cooing and whining and grunting and squealing together. So he looked upstream, and there he saw an equally extraordinary sight—a sort of glassy fur ball, all shiny with water, that was rolling toward them, and sometimes broke up and streamed on in separate shapes, and then joined up again; and the closer it got, the louder the noise it made.

The dragonfly couldn't see it at all from that distance, so Tom dived off the leaf and struck out to have a closer look for himself. What did he find but several beautiful creatures, all rolling and wrestling and biting and hugging and plunging and fighting—and all much, much bigger than he was!

Unluckily for him, the largest spotted him at once. She cried out, "Look, children—look what we've got for dinner!" and came straight at him. She had such wicked eyes, and such sharp teeth in her grinning mouth, that Tom whisked in between some strong water-lily roots, and made faces at her.

"Come out this instant," hissed the otter. "Do as you're told, or you'll regret it!"

But Tom shook the roots at her, and made his worst faces. (It was what he used to do to old women in his other life, through the city railings.)

"Dear me, children," said the otter haughtily. "It is not fit to eat, after all. It is only a revolting little newt."

"I'm not a newt," said Tom. "Newts have tails."

"You have hands, so you must have a tail. You're a newt."

Tom turned around then, so she could see that he had no tail. She could have called him a frog, but she made it a rule never to contradict herself. "I see you are a newt, and there's no point in denying it. You are not fit for my children and me to eat, I shall leave you to the salmon. They'll gobble you up quick enough!" And she laughed. Otters can laugh. It is not a pleasant noise.

"What are salmon?" asked Tom in alarm.

"Salmon are fish, little newt, great big fish, a hundred times bigger than you are! They call themselves the lords of the river, but we rule the salmon. We hunt them from pool to pool, and corner them, and then, my dear little newt, we bite out their throats!" She said this with such a greedy grin, and such an evil expression, that Tom was disgusted. "They'll soon be here. I can smell rain coming off the sea, and then hurrah for the floods and the salmon, and won't we make pigs of ourselves!"

All the otters began turning somersaults at the thought, and the old otter stood up and looked right out of the stream, grinning like a Cheshire cat.

"Where do the salmon come from?" asked Tom. He was keeping well in among the roots, for he was very afraid of these beautiful, bloodthirsty creatures.

"Out of the sea, my newt! Out of the great, wide, shining sea! Oh, there is nothing like the seaside for a family holiday! I don't suppose you've ever been there? It's such good fishing, and we play in the breakers, and sleep soundly among the warm dry rocks. But men ruin it, of course. Men always spoil everything!"

"What are men?" asked Tom. And yet, in some strange way, he seemed to know what men were.

"Dear me, how ignorant you are! But there, you're a newt and can't help it. Men are two-legged things, newt, with arms and hands—in fact something like you, only much bigger and they haven't got tails. They are too clumsy to catch fish as we do, they have to use hooks and lines, and they set pots for lobsters. They killed my darling husband as he was hunting for something for us to eat—I was sheltering with the children in the rocks, because the sea was so rough. He gave up his life for his family; no husband could do more. Poor dear, obedient hero that he was! Alas, alas!" and the otter was so stricken by her memories that she swam slowly away downstream, with her children following in stately procession, like boats around a liner.

But Tom stayed hidden in the roots, because at that moment half a dozen little terriers came running down the bank, barking and yelping and scuttering in the water. He couldn't know that these were really the water fairies, who had been listening to the conversation, and thought he had talked enough to the dangerous otters.

Now the summer was nearly over. At last a day came so stiflingly hot that even the stream felt tepid. The trout had no energy to take any flies. Tom wriggled in between their cool sides and wondered, in a soporific way, what was going to happen. For there was a general feeling of apprehension, even under the water—a sense that everything was holding its breath.

Toward evening, the sky grew unnaturally dark, and a bank of clouds lowered over the valley. Now everything kept perfectly still, even Tom peeping out from the water. Nothing stirred—not a breath of wind; there was no sound, not even from the smallest bird. Everything was transfixed . . . waiting. . . .

Plop—plop—some large drops of rain hit the water. One landed on Tom's nose, and he ducked into the pool—just in time. The first flash of lightning leapt across Vendale, slicing from cliff to cliff, and in the same instant there was a thunderclap like the end of the world.

It started to rain in earnest, rain in bucketfuls, which dashed Tom to the bank, and churned the stream into a torrent. He hid behind a boulder and watched wide-eyed the tide of sticks and old nests, addled eggs, beetles, woodlice, worms—all whirling helter-skelter at breakneck speed. And suddenly, the trout came to life. They darted to and fro like flashes of quicksilver, gobbling the insects as they hurtled down and quarreling over the best bits.

The lightning was so powerful that it lit the stream to the very bottom as clear as day. Tom looked down through the mud and gasped. It was alive with eels, all writhing and twisting. They had lived all summer down there, in burrows or cool cracks in the rocks. He had only ever seen one or two, at night. But here they were in quantities, heaving along the bottom, and crowding and twining so swiftly that he was afraid. As they swarmed past, he could hear them muttering in deep, muddy voices, "Hooray for a thunderstorm at last! Down to the sea, boys, down to the sea!"

The otters came after the eels. Tom hoped the old mother wouldn't see him, but she did. "Come along, little newt!" she cried out. "What are you doing, hiding there? Don't you want to see the world? Hurry, hurry, my children—succulent salmon for breakfast!" And they swept on and away.

Then came a flash of lightning so brilliant that all the water around him turned white for a second, and in that flash he saw—he was certain he saw—three beautiful girls with their arms around each other's necks, borne on the rush of the stream. They were gone in an instant, but he heard them singing, "Down to the sea, down to the sea!"

"Oh, wait!" cried poor Tom. "Please! Wait for me!" Their sweet voices still reached him through the tumult of thunder and rain.

He made up his mind. "Down to the sea!" he shouted, and he leapt bravely into the furious current. "Goodbye, trout!" But their mouths were too full to answer.

Tom was snatched and whirled along on the torrent between the familiar banks, and soon between banks he didn't know at all. There was no point in trying to swim. He was carried past dark villages where all the windows and curtains had been shut tight against the storm. He was swept under dark bridges, bounced down waterfalls, and rolled through narrow places, till he thought there was no breath left in his body. No way could he stop, but he wouldn't have anyhow, for he was part of the great tide of water and water creatures all rushing to the sea!

Chapter Eight

At last the storm subsided, and it was dawn. Where was Tom then? The stream that ran through Vendale turned at last into a river—the broad salmon river, where the water moved slow and stately, even after such a storm. It was so wide that, when he put out his head to look, he could hardly see the opposite bank.

"So this must be the sea," he said to himself, rather nervously. "What a huge place! If I go any further I'm sure to get lost, or something savage will eat me."

He crept among the rocks and waited hopefully for a friendly creature, but none came. At last, feeling anxious and dispirited, and very tired besides after his journey, he fell asleep.

When he woke, he looked around—and his heart gave a thump! What a fish! It was a hundred—a thousand times as big as he was! Why, a trout was a midget by comparison! It was all silver from its hooked nose to its tail, with a curling lip and a disdainful eye. Surely, this must be a salmon!

Tom stared at it and kept perfectly still, for he remembered what the otter had said, and he was afraid he was going to be eaten. However, the salmon sailed past with a swish of its tail. Presently came another, then more together, sometimes leaping clean out of the water for joy so that their silver bodies gleamed in the sun, and rushing up the river as if they were coming home.

The last of the salmon was bigger than all the others, but not joyful. He had a careworn expression, and Tom saw that he had his wife with him.

"My sweet," he heard the salmon say lovingly, "I don't like to see you so exhausted. Let us rest here a little," and he nudged her toward the rocks where Tom was sitting. Then he noticed him and looked suddenly fierce.

"Oh, don't be angry with me!" cried Tom. "I won't be any trouble!"

"I beg your pardon," said the fish in a kinder tone. "I have met several of your sort before. Please excuse us for intruding on your privacy. As soon as my wife has recovered her strength, we will leave you in peace. How are you feeling now, my love?" he asked his companion tenderly, stroking her with his fin.

But there was a question Tom couldn't wait to ask. "You mean you've seen creatures like me before—water babies?"

"Indeed yes—in the sea. Only last evening one came to warn us of some nets staked out across the river. He guided us around them in the most courteous way."

"Water babies in the sea!" cried Tom, with shining eyes. "Oh! That will be better than playing with caddises and trout!"

"Trout!" the lady salmon repeated faintly, with a shudder. "You played with trout! How too appalling! The very idea makes me giddy."

"Spare yourself, my darling," urged the tender husband. "Don't endanger your health by considering it for a moment."

"But it was good fun," protested Tom, feeling he should be loyal to his old friends.

"I have to admit that the trout are relations of ours," the salmon told him. "Long, long ago, they chose to stay in the streams instead of going boldly down to the great wide sea to grow strong and large, as we do. No, they preferred to poke about and gobble worms and maggots. . . ."

"And look how hideously ugly they've become!" his wife interrupted, hysterically. "All small and vulgar and spotted! And they have simply no idea of their social status—simply no idea . . ." her voice trembled with emotion.

"Be calm, be calm, my love!" begged her husband.

"Why, I even heard of one who proposed marriage to a salmon!" she finished with a shriek.

"If ever I met such an upstart, I should kill him instantly," said her husband, with a curl of his lip.

This promise seemed to soothe the lady salmon, and soon after they moved upstream side by side; not before Tom had warned them about the savage otters. He went on alone down the river, keeping close to the shore. He meant to find the sea, but it was a long, long way, and the journey took many days.

Now that summer was over, the river would have felt cold to a human child, but Tom minded it no more than a fish. During his solitary traveling, he looked about him at the country he passed, at the smoky towns he could see from the river, and the fine houses with great trees and lawns stretching down to the water, and he wondered what kinds of creatures lived in these different places. At night he found a safe hole in the rocks, where he slept and dreamed strange dreams. And then one night he had a terrible adventure.

The moon was full, so bright that it shone through the water where Tom was trying to sleep, as if it was calling him to show him something. At last he uncurled and let himself float to the surface and climbed up onto a rock. He stared at the moon, and it stared back at him, like a round yellow eye in the middle of the night. He watched how its light rippled on the river, and looked across at the fields all pale and silvery with dew, and the silhouettes of the trees. Everything was so still that he could smell their piney scent, and the sweetness of heather wafting down from the moor, and hear exactly what the owls were saying to each other. He sat there for a long time, quite lost in peace and beauty, like a little night bird himself.

Then he saw a smoky red light moving along the riverbank. Every now and then it paused and pointed into the water, which it seemed to pierce with flame. Tom had never seen anything like it, and he slid quietly down and swam close to find out what it could be.

The light had stopped now on the edge. Under its beam Tom was astonished to see several large salmon in the shallows of the river, goggling at it as if they couldn't look at anything else, and waggling their tails with pleasure.

So he thought he would try to find out what was making this bewitching light, and rising to the top, he broke the surface of the water with a splash. At once he heard a gruff voice mutter, much too close, "There's another."

Now he didn't understand what that meant, but he seemed to know the voice that spoke. There on the bank were three huge creatures, each standing on two legs. One was holding the light, which flared and sputtered, and another had a long pole. And somehow, he knew that these were men, and he

was so frightened that his heart began to race; but he ducked down and hid himself among the rocks, to see what happened next.

The man carrying the torch was peering into the water, and then he pointed and whispered to the man beside him with the pole, "That's our boy—fifteen pounds if he's an ounce! Mind how you go!"

The silly salmon were still goggling at the light. Tom was suddenly sure that harm was coming to them, and he wondered how he could warn them without being seen. Too late! Zap! The pole split the water, there was a frenzy of splashing and thrashing, and—alas!—in a twinkling the largest of the salmon was hoisted out onto the bank, speared clean through with the pole.

But three gamekeepers had been creeping up in the darkness, and at that moment they sprang on the salmon poachers. Then there was such a fight— such crashes and thumps and shouting and swearing—that Tom turned white with terror at the sound. He could see the men struggling by the scarlet light of the torch, and the rocks where he was hiding shook with the trampling of feet. Then there was a tremendous splash, and a hiss, and the light went out.

The man holding the torch had been knocked into the water. The others ran up and down the bank in the dark trying to find him, but in vain. At last they gave it up and went away, the three keepers with two poachers and a speared salmon between them. But the third poacher had sunk to the bottom of a deep pool. He lay there, perfectly still.

Tom waited a long time before he ventured out of his hiding place. He could see the man, palely lit by the rippling moon—he seemed to be asleep. He swam around him, keeping a safe distance. The man never moved. Perhaps the water has sent him to sleep, Tom thought; perhaps he will wake up a water baby like me. He swam a little closer; there was something familiar about the man. He swam closer yet, till he could see his face staring sightlessly up through the water at the moon. He looked full at him—and suddenly he remembered. He knew this man. It was Grimes.

Tom spun around and swam away at top speed. Memories of his old life came crowding back—oh, if Grimes was turned into a water baby, what a horrible one he would be!

Poor little Tom spent the rest of the night hidden close under the bank. Next morning, he peered out anxiously, but everything looked just as usual. So he told himself that it had all been a dream, but still he thought he would go and have another look—just quickly—just to make sure. So he set off very cautiously, hiding under roots and peeping around rocks, till he came to the pool. Grimes was still lying there. Then he knew that it hadn't been a dream, and he dashed away, quite terrified, and sick at heart because his lovely underwater life had been spoiled.

That afternoon he went back again with a thumping heart, and this time the pool was empty. Grimes had gone. Now Tom was certain he had been turned into a water baby, and he hurried away and went on down the river as fast as he could, because he was so afraid of meeting him.

Chapter Nine

Down to the sea, down to the sea! But how sad the country looked to him now, with the leaves all brown and red and yellow, drifting into the river as the autumn wind whirled them from the trees! Sometimes a white mist shrouded the hills, sometimes it lay so thick across the water that he couldn't see where he was going. Then he trusted the current; and so he went down, day after day, under huge bridges, past a great town with mills and docks and barges moored, and ships at anchor, and rubbish all over the river. When he saw sailors lounging, smoking on the decks of the ships, he ducked at once, with his heart pounding. If only he could have known that the water fairies were always there to look after him, how comforted he would have been!

At last the day came when he caught sight of a bright red object bobbing far ahead in the middle of the water. This was the buoy that marked the river entrance, and soon he found that the current which had been taking him down changed abruptly and tried to take him up instead.

It was the tide, of course, but Tom hadn't heard about tides. He simply found that the fresh water all around him had turned to salt. And then he felt marvelous! He felt so good that he jumped clean out of the water three times, head over heels, in a way that would have done credit to a trout! He kept his eyes on the scarlet buoy dancing on the waves, and he struck out for it.

He passed a great many fish coming in to feast on shrimps, and then he met a seal who was hungrily following the fish. This seal was as long as a dinghy, and as shiny as if he had been done all over with boot polish. He winked at Tom with his bleary bulbous eyes, and said in his treacly voice, "Hallo, my little fellow. If you are looking for your brothers and sisters, I saw them playing further out."

This was wonderful news! Tom swam on faster than ever, and soon he reached the buoy and clambered onto it. He sat there, rocking on the waves, and scanned the sea in all directions. But—he couldn't see any water babies.

The water in the bay was as blue as the sky, and lined with a strip of white sand. The waves met the sand in a curl of foam, or broke upon the rocks in feathers of spray. The air tasted of salt and rang with the cries of the gulls, who hovered over Tom on his perch. He was rather nervous of them at first, but they did him no harm. So he called, "Excuse me! Have you seen any water babies?" But they didn't answer, while they marked time with their wide, white wings.

The water babies must be there, if the seal had seen them! Tom dived off the buoy and swam all around. He thought he could hear them laughing—but it was only the noise of the waves. Then he was sure he saw them playing in the sand on the bottom. He plunged down to join them with a happy heart—and found a handful of pink and white shells.

So poor Tom sat on the seabed and howled with grief and disappointment.

They must be there, so why didn't they come out? They didn't want to play with him, that must be the answer, and it made Tom miserable. Perhaps the ones along the shore were more friendly. He left the buoy and swam to the rocks and searched there. He hunted under the wet seaweed, and in the evenings he wandered over the sand, but still he couldn't find them. "Where are you? Oh please, please come!" he called out in his loneliness. But if he heard an answering voice, it was only a bird, or an echo.

However, he found one friend among the rocks. This was a lobster so ancient that he had barnacles living on his claws. What an extraordinary animal! He looked more like a machine than a creature. He had often seen water babies, and he didn't like them. They were silly little things who couldn't even grow a shell on their backs, and they went about helping silly fish, which was a complete waste of time.

"I should be ashamed to need help from a little softy like you," he told Tom, rudely. "At my age I can look after myself, I hope!"

He was certainly not a humble or even an amiable old lobster. But he looked so funny, and his habits were so odd, and Tom was so lonely that they became friends and used to sit in two holes, side by side, and have long conversations together.

And now something happened to Tom that was of the greatest importance, and so dangerous, that it nearly put an end to his search for the water babies.

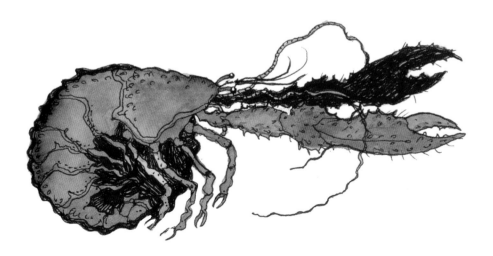

Chapter Ten

Now it was winter. Cold winds blew in from the sea, and the moors over Vendale were singed brown by the frost. At Harthover Place, Sir John went out hunting three days a week. He didn't come home until dusk, when he would gobble his dinner and slump down in his armchair in front of the fire and snore out the evening.

"Dear me," said his wife, in the chair opposite. "So you had a good day?"

Mumble grunt.

"The children are looking pale—I wonder whether the sea air would do them good. I think perhaps a few days at the seaside. . . ."

Sn-o-o-re, snort. Some soot fell down the chimney.

"Really I might as well go," said his wife, tartly. "At this time of year you hardly notice whether I am here or not!"

So the nurse packed some trunks of warm clothes, and she set off the next day with the children and a party of friends. They rented a house overlooking the sea—as luck would have it, not more than a mile from the very place where Tom liked to sit with the lobster.

And one dry, cold, windy afternoon, Ellie went out for a walk. A friend of her father's came with her. He was a professor, and he liked Ellie because she listened to him politely. As they walked along the shore, she would stop and fish the rock pools, and he would then describe, very carefully and accurately, what she had caught. He showed her all the different kinds of seaweed and explained them patiently in simple language, and picked the living creatures out of the net with his thin yellow fingers, and peered down his long nose at them, and gave them complicated names that no one could possibly remember. At last poor Ellie felt so tired that she exclaimed, "It's so boring! How can it be so boring? I wish I could catch a water baby!"

"A water baby? My dear little Ellie, what a perfectly charming idea! But of course there's no such thing as a water baby."

"How do you know?" said Ellie, rudely, and threw down her net on the sand.

This upset the professor. He had been enjoying his walk, and he liked educating people when they were very young and treated him with respect. He nearly snapped at her; however he bent down instead and picked up the net and jabbed it under the seaweed. As he pulled it out, he noticed that it was heavy, so he lifted it quickly and there, all entangled, lay struggling Tom.

"Well, well!" exclaimed the professor. "This is an unusually large holothurian—and look here, my dear Ellie, do you see—it has hands! Can it be related to synapta?"

He unwound the net and picked out Tom between his fingers.

"It has eyes! This is really most exciting! It must be a cephalopod! Look, Ellie!"

Then Ellie did look at Tom, and immediately shrieked, "It's a water baby!"

"Rubbish," said the professor, reaching for the little bucket they had brought with them. "Everyone knows they don't exist," and he gave Tom a poke.

Now Tom had been keeping perfectly still, though he was pale with dread. For he had a terrible feeling that if a man caught him, he would be somehow turned into a chimney sweep again, and be all dirty and miserable. But when he was poked, it was more than he could stand, and he put his face to the bony yellow finger, and bit it with all his strength.

The professor yelled with pain and dropped Tom like a hot potato. He hit the seaweed, slipped into the water, and disappeared in an instant.

"It was a water baby, and you let it go!" cried Ellie, bursting into tears. She jumped down onto the seaweed after Tom, but she was wearing leather boots because it was so cold, and—alas!—she slipped and fell. She hit her head on a rock and lay still.

The poor, silly professor was dreadfully upset. He washed her face with saltwater, and rubbed her hands, and called her name tenderly over and over again, but she wouldn't wake up. So at last he lifted her gently in his arms and took her home, all pale and limp. And the net and the little bucket waited on the sand until the tide carried them away.

Ellie was put to bed, and hot-water bottles were brought, and the doctor was called, but nothing could be done. She was in such a deep sleep that no one could wake her. Once or twice she babbled about water babies, but no one understood what she meant. Except the professor—but he said nothing, because he felt so ashamed.

So a whole week passed, very sadly, until one night the fairies came to visit Ellie. They brought with them a pair of beautiful wings, and they woke her up and showed her how to put them on. Then they all flew away together— far, far away. And Ellie was completely well again; but nobody saw her for a long time.

Chapter Eleven

Tom was not hurt when the professor dropped him. He landed on a mattress of seaweed, dived straight into the water, and swam till he could swim no more. Then he crept among the rocks and lay there for a long time, quite breathless, and still trembling every now and then with fright.

At first he could only remember how the professor's eyes had glittered, horribly enlarged by his spectacles. It was a nightmare, which made him shudder. But as he grew calmer, he began to think about the little girl with golden hair.

He wondered who she was, and why he had the feeling that he had seen her before. She was so pretty! Poor, lonely Tom longed to have her as a friend, to play with.

He came out from the rocks, and swam to a safe distance, and looked back along the shore. She had gone, and so had the tall, thin man. Perhaps she would come again tomorrow, perhaps she would be alone, and he would be able to talk to her. His heart filled with happy dreams. He thought he would tell the lobster about it, and he swam toward the rocks where they sat together. The water here was very deep and clear, and shoals of fish were sculling about, eating the prawns and barnacles. He was watching them when he noticed a round cage made of willow stakes. It was the first he had seen, and he dived down to investigate it. What was this! His friend the lobster was sitting inside, quite pink with embarrassment and frustration!

"What are you doing in there?" cried Tom in astonishment.

The old creature was too depressed to make excuses. He growled, "I can't get out."

"Why did you go in?"

"After that disgusting old fish." The lobster had thought the bait quite

delicious, but now he found himself trapped in the lobster pot; even the smell of it made him sick.

"Why don't you get out the way you got in, through the round spiky hole at the top?"

"Do you think I haven't tried? I've jumped every which way, but I can't find the hole."

Tom looked carefully at the trap, and then he said, "If you turn your back to me, I'll pull you out, and then you won't get hung up on the spikes."

So the lobster tried, but he was so large that he couldn't contrive to aim himself backward at the hole. Tom braced himself at the opening and, reaching in, grabbed him by the tail. But his friend was in such a muddle and a panic, he pulled Tom in after him!

"What did you go and do that for?" exclaimed Tom in exasperation. "Never mind," he added quickly, seeing that the lobster was close to despair. "I tell you what, if you break off the spikes with your huge claws, we'll both get out without any trouble."

"Of course, of course!" cried the foolish old creature. "Why didn't I think of it?" and he began to break off the spikes.

But then—oh, horror!—something like a dark cloud moved in over them. The head of the cloud split into a grin with teeth, and Tom was dismayed to see the otter.

"Ha-ha!" she exclaimed like an ogress, as soon as she spied Tom in the trap. "Now I've got you! Shan't I pay you out for telling the salmon about me!" And she started to creep all over the pot, looking for the way in.

Now Tom thought his end had come, for she soon found the hole and squeezed herself through it, all eyes and teeth. But as she came in, the intrepid lobster snapped her by the nose, and no matter how she writhed and screamed, he held on.

So there they were, all three, tightly crammed into the pot. The otter tore at the lobster, but he gripped her bravely like a vice, and the pot rocked to and fro, and poor Tom had all the breath knocked out of him. At last he had a chance to climb on top of the otter and get out through the hole.

He could have swum away then, but he intended to save his friend, so he stuck his feet firmly between the fastenings of the trap, and as soon as the lobster's tail came up, he grabbed it, and heaved with all his strength. But the lobster held on to the otter.

"Let go, let go!" shouted Tom. "She's dead, can't you see?"

And she was—drowned dead. That was the end of her.

But then the worst thing happened. The rope attached to the lobster pot quivered and went taut. A fisherman in a boat had begun hauling it to the surface.

"Come on, you silly old fool!" shouted Tom in desperation. "Do you want to be caught by a fisherman?"

But still the lobster held on to the otter. And the greeny-blue sea got lighter and lighter as the pot slowly rose to the surface.

Now there was nothing more that Tom could do. He floated off and watched in despair as the lobster pot, with the lobster and the otter in it, was hauled up to the boat. This was the end, he thought. But, no! Just as the fisherman was landing the pot, the lobster realized what was happening, and with one tremendous snap, he leapt from the pot, out of the fisherman's clutch, and—splash! back into the sea. But he left his great knobby claw behind him, because even then he couldn't bring himself to let go of the wicked otter.

Just five minutes later, Tom found his first water baby.

The little fellow was sitting on the sand, replanting some seaweed and anemones that had been washed away by a storm. As soon as he saw Tom, he jumped up and exclaimed, "What's this? A new water baby!"

"Here you are at last!" cried Tom. "I've been searching for you everywhere!"

"We've been here ages—hundreds of us all around the shore. You must have seen us or heard us shouting to each other!"

Tom looked him in the face and suddenly said, "I do believe you're right. I have seen you, often and often, but I didn't know it."

"You can help me if you like," said the water baby, catching at a handful of loose seaweed, and patting the roots into a hole he quickly dug in the sand. "That last storm made an awful mess. I want to finish this bit of gardening before the others come back and we have to go home."

So Tom dug and his new friend planted seaweed until the turn of the tide. Then they were suddenly surrounded by a crowd of water babies. They were all shouting and laughing and singing in the surf, and Tom had often heard them before, but thought it was only the rippling of the sea. They set off for home, plunging and skimming through the sea like a shoal of jolly little fish; but Tom was the happiest of them all.

The home of the water babies lay under a magical island, far out in the western sea. It was a holy place. Once upon a time, monks had lived on the island, and they slept there still, lulled by the waves, and the wind in the pine trees, and the wailing of the gulls.

The island was supported on great rocky pillars, all brightly colored—some shiny black, some striped green and crimson, or red or yellow or sparkling white. Between them, on the sea bottom, there were caves where the water babies slept, on beds of the softest white sand. The curtains were made of seaweed, green and brown, crimson and purple. The sand was spotlessly clean, and the water as clear as crystal, for crabs and corals and anemones collected any dirt, which was food to them. These creatures clung to the rocks in brilliant colors and patterns, like bunches of underwater flowers.

Thousands of sea snakes kept watch over this place by day and by night, in case anything came that might be harmful. They had extra eyes in their tails, and were well-armed with cutters and mincers and stabbers, so they made excellent guardians.

Little Tom had been the loneliest water baby on the shore. Now his dream

had come true—he was surrounded by hundreds of children just like himself. He had friends to play with and things to do every minute of the day, and he should have been perfectly happy.

But, alas! Instead of working and playing with the other children in this beautiful place, what must he do, in a day or two, but go back to his old habits! He did not tease the water snakes—he was too afraid of them. But he ran at the crabs to make them hide under the sand with just their eyes peeping out—he thought this extremely funny; and he pushed pebbles into the sea anemones' mouths, which gave them indigestion.

His friends saw him at his tricks and warned him to stop it. "Mrs. Bedonebyasyoudid is coming," they said. "You'll be sorry then."

"Why? You aren't sneaks, are you?"

"No, but she knows everything that happens here. You'd better be careful!"

But Tom didn't care about Mrs. Bedonebyasyoudid, or anyone else for that matter. He was too full of high spirits. And then, early on Friday morning, this lady made her weekly visit.

Chapter Twelve

Mrs. Bedonebyasyoudid was very tall, and very old, and very severe, with thick eyebrows, and a rather bristly jaw. Her nose was hooked like a beak, and on it balanced a pair of green spectacles. She was dressed all in black, with long sleeves and a shawl, and a gloomy black bonnet. Altogether, she was so exceedingly ugly that Tom was tempted to make faces at her; but he didn't, because under her arm she carried a birch rod.

As soon as she came, the children pushed back their hair and stood in a line. "Good morning, Mrs. Bedonebyasyoudid," they said in a chorus, politely.

She walked down the line, looking carefully at each child, and seemed pleased with them all. Then she gave each one a treat—a sea biscuit, sea mint, sea chocolate, sea lollipop; and to the very best she gave sea ices, made of sea cow's cream, more delicious than anything on earth.

Tom was the last child in the line. He watched the treats being given out and his mouth watered, and his eyes grew round with longing. What would she give him? Oh, might it be a sea ice, because he was a new water baby? At last his turn came. He shut his eyes and opened his mouth, and the lady put in his reward. Not a sea ice—not even a sea mint! She gave him a hard, cold stone.

Tom spat it out, and started to cry. "That's not fair," he snuffled, knuckling his eyes.

"Were you being fair when you gave the anemones pebbles to eat and made them ill? What you did to them, I must do to you. It is my function in life."

"It was only a game. How should I know?" whined Tom.

"Well, now you do! You see," said the old lady, looking at him piercingly through her green spectacles, "if you do something wrong, you will be punished for it, sooner or later."

"Well, I think you are very unkind," whimpered Tom.

"Not a bit of it. I am your best friend, even though it is my business to punish you. I don't like doing it, but I can't help it. I am like a machine full of cogs and springs, wound up to do what I have to do, to make you good and happy."

"Were you really wound up? Was it a long time ago?" For Tom thought, 'she'll run down, like Mr. Grimes's watch that he used to forget to wind when he was drunk, and then I'll be free!'

But the lady knew exactly what was going through his mind.
She said, "I was wound up when the first person was born, and I shall go on working for as long as the last person." And then she looked up, up—beyond the pillars, and the island, and the sea—and she smiled, so that Tom, who was staring at her, suddenly saw that she wasn't ugly at all.

He smiled at her then, and she looked down at him and said, "You see, I'm not as ugly as you thought. And one day, when all the people in the world are good, I shall be as beautiful as my sister, Mrs. Doasyouwouldbedoneby. You'll meet her soon, and you'll love her—all children do! But now I must get on with my work. You can all run away," she said to the water babies, who were still standing respectfully around her. "But not you, Tom. You must stay and watch me. It will be a useful lesson to you before you go to school."

So all the children swam away, and Tom was left alone with the old lady, wondering anxiously what she was going to do.

"Now, little Tom," she said kindly, "every Friday I come here to see all the people who have been unkind to children, and I do exactly the same to them."

Tom was so scared that he hid under a stone, disturbing two crabs and a flatfish.

So first Mrs. Bedonebyasyoudid called for all the irresponsible doctors and gave them the wrong medicines, so that their heads ached and they got pains in their insides. Next, it was the turn of silly parents, aunts, uncles, grannies, and careless girls who were supposed to look after children but took no trouble. They were smacked and shouted at, and stuffed with sweets, and scalded with hot tea.

All this led to much shouting and tears, but Mrs. Bedonebyasyoudid took no notice. By the time she had finished with them, she was so tired that she took an hour off for lunch.

During the afternoon, she called in all the bad schoolteachers. She boxed their ears and accused them of not knowing their lessons. At last she beat them all with her birch rod, and gave them punishments of extra homework that must be learned by next Friday, and sent them away howling so loudly that the sea all around the island was full of bubbles.

It was all very alarming to Tom, who peeped out from under the rock with his heart beating fast. But sometimes the old lady glanced at him, and then she didn't look angry—indeed, sometimes she smiled. So when everyone had gone away, and she was straightening her bonnet and smoothing her gown and retying her shawl before going home, he dared to come out and ask her a question.

"Excuse me," he began, very politely.

"What is it, my little dear?"

"What about my old master, Grimes? Why don't you punish him? He used to be horrible to me."

Then he wished he hadn't asked, because the old lady suddenly looked so grim. She said, "You can be sure I am looking after him, and all the others like him. The people you saw today were only silly and impatient. But Grimes and the rest are in quite a different place. They have been really wicked, because they knew quite well that they were doing wrong."

Now there was something in her voice that brought Tom out in goose pimples all over.

"There, there," said the old lady, more cheerfully. "Don't bother your little head about him any more. Just be a good boy and stop teasing those poor creatures. And then you'll have a happy time with my beautiful sister, Mrs. Doasyouwouldbedoneby. She visits every Sunday." With these words she gave him a brisk tap on the head that made him blink, and went away.

Tom was very glad to hear that there was no chance of meeting Mr. Grimes, but he couldn't help thinking how awful it must be to be looked after by that fierce old lady. He was careful not to chase any crabs or pretend he had dinner for the anemones. And sure enough, two days later, Mrs. Doasyouwouldbedoneby came to spend Sunday with the water babies.

She was as tall as her sister but quite different. She was so pretty and

smiling and kind and loving, that as soon as the children saw her they all
began dancing and singing and turning somersaults and doing handstands for
joy, and as soon as she sat down they rushed at her, and sat on her knee, and
climbed on her shoulders, and hugged her and kissed her, so that her beautiful
long hair came unplaited and her loving arms were full of children. And the
ones without any room on her lap or in her arms swarmed around her feet and
legs—so that she was almost covered with water babies.

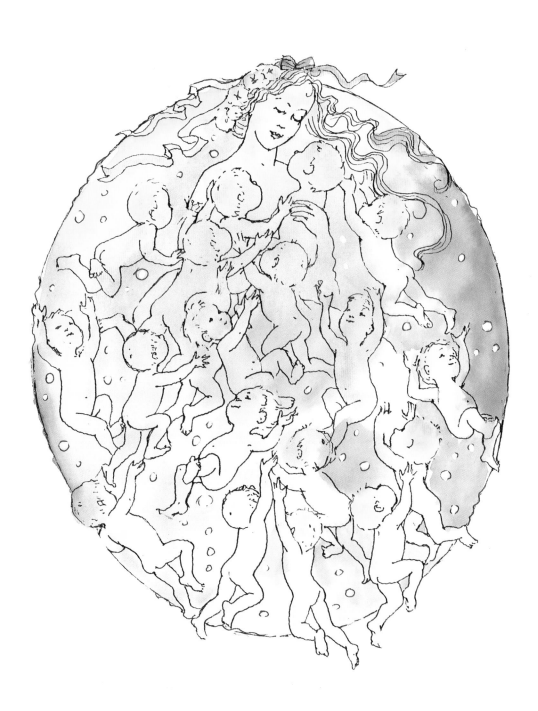

Only Tom stood and stared at them. He didn't understand what love was, because he had never had any.

But Mrs. Doasyouwouldbedoneby noticed him at once, and she cried out, "Why, you are a new baby—how exciting!" Then she lifted off armfuls of children to make room for him, and putting him on her lap, bent over him and hugged him, while the others came scrambling and crowding back until they covered her from head to foot. But she talked quietly to Tom while he looked at her face and loved her because she was so kind and good. He looked, and listened, and loved until he fell asleep.

When he woke up, she was telling the children the story that began on the first Christmas Day. The only sound in that beautiful place was her voice describing this good man's life, and Tom listened with the others, wondering about it. After a while he went back to sleep, and this time, when he woke, she was singing. Her voice was as gentle as the sea on a soft day, and the song she sang was very sweet. When she had finished, she said, "Oh dear, I shall have to go in a minute." Then she turned to Tom. "Now, you will be good, won't you, till I come back next Sunday?"

"And I can sit here again, and you will hug me again?"

"Of course I will, little darling! I wish I could take you with me and keep you in my arms all the time, but I can't."

So the beautiful lady went away, and it seemed to the children a very long time till next Sunday. But her visit had warmed Tom's heart, and after that he never teased anything again.

Chapter Thirteen

It was stormy that spring, and there was plenty of work for the water babies to do. Every day they swam to the shore to put back the plants that had been swept away, and clean out the rock pools, and give directions to confused birds who had been blown off course, and bewildered fish. Tom worked as hard as anyone and took his place in the line every Friday, when he got his reward from Mrs. Bedonebyasyoudid.

Those sea sweets were so delicious! He always hoped she'd give him an extra one, for being so particularly good—but she never did. He thought about them, and longed for them more and more. He even dreamed sweets at night—especially the sea ice cream.

He wondered where she kept all those tempting things. She didn't bring them with her—she only carried a birch rod. There must be a box hidden somewhere. He kept an eye out for it when he was playing games under the island with the other children. He hunted for it whenever he was alone. Oh, he was ashamed of himself—but he couldn't help it—the sweets were so nice! But the box was so cleverly hidden that he couldn't find it.

So then he began following Mrs. Bedonebyasyoudid, to see where she took them from and where she hid them away. If she looked at him, he pretended to be busy doing something else. He became very clever at spying on her, but he was stupid as well—he should have remembered that she could read his thoughts. And at last he did discover where she kept the sweets. They were stored in a beautiful pearly chest in a deep crack between the rocks.

Now poor Tom was exceedingly miserable. He longed to go and look at them—only *look*—but he was too frightened. He did look at them in his dreams, and woke up feeling guilty. So at last he said to himself, "I might as well go. Anyway, it can't be wrong—just to *look*."

So one night, when the seaweed curtains were drawn, and all the children were fast asleep on their sandy beds, Tom crept out. He was very nervous of the water snakes, but they took no notice of him. He stole to the rocky crevice with his heart beating hard. He took a deep breath and dived in. It was as dark as a chimney. There at the bottom glowed the pearly box. He swam all around it, in case there was a water snake. He thought, I bet she keeps it locked.

He tried the lid. It opened easily. Oh, Tom! There were all the treats arranged inside, and he longed and longed, and stared and stared at them, and felt horribly afraid, but not enough to slam the lid and dash away. His greed was greater than his fear. He thought, I'll just touch one—that can't be wrong—just to *touch*.

So he touched one, and then he took it out, and then it was somehow in his mouth, and he swallowed it so quickly, he could hardly taste it. Well, that was a terrible thing to do—to steal sweets—especially from such a lady as Mrs. Bedonebyasyoudid! But if he had eaten one, why not two? So he took another, and then another, and then he thought, what if she comes in and catches me? So he began snatching and gobbling so fast that he felt sick, but even that didn't stop him. He kept at it, trembling with fear and greed, and soon the box was empty.

He didn't know it, but Mrs. Bedonebyasyoudid was standing just behind him all the time.

First she took off her spectacles, as if she really couldn't bear to look at what was happening. Next she raised her bushy eyebrows almost into her hair, and her large eyes, that could look so fierce, filled with tears. Did she dash at Tom with her birch rod? No. She simply said, in a very mournful tone, "Oh dear, oh dear. You are exactly the same as the others." But Tom couldn't hear what she said, and he couldn't see her, either. When the box was empty, he crept away to bed. He felt wretched, and he was sick during the night.

Next day, he lined up with the other children for her inspection. He was so frightened that he shook all over, but he was more frightened to hide in case she came looking for him. Worst of all, he was afraid there would be no sweets—after all, he had finished everything in her box!

But no, she produced as many as ever. When it was his turn, she looked at him searchingly, and he trembled but said nothing.

She gave him his sweet, and he thought, "She doesn't know it was me."

The sweet—a sea biscuit—tasted disgusting. It gave him a pain for the rest of the week, and made him angry and miserable.

When Mrs. Doasyouwouldbedoneby came on Sunday, he tried to climb onto her knee. But she said gently, "I wish I could give you a hug, but I can't. I'm afraid you're too prickly!"

That was a shock. He looked down at himself—it was true! His nice smooth water-baby skin was covered all over with sharp little spines.

Then he was dreadfully ashamed. He went away on his own, and sulked and cried. He didn't join in any games, he didn't even go to work with the others. He hid himself as much as possible, and the days passed drearily until Mrs. Bedonebyasyoudid came.

He stood in the line of children, and this time he suddenly couldn't bear it any longer. He blurted out what he had done, and cried bitterly while he waited for her to attack him with her birch rod.

But she didn't. Instead, she put her long thin arms around him and gave him a bristly kiss. "That's right!" she exclaimed, and her eyes looked very bright through her green spectacles. "All forgiven! Because you have told the truth!"

"But what about my prickles?" sobbed Tom. "Oh please, take them away! I'm so lonely and so unhappy—even worse than I was before!"

"Dear me! But I can't do that," said the old lady. "You made those prickles grow, and only you can get rid of them."

"But I don't know how!"

"Of course you don't! You have to be taught. I shall fetch you a schoolmistress, and she will tell you what to do."

This idea filled Tom with dread. He could only hope that the teacher would be very old and very kind—like the one in Vendale.

But when she came, she was quite, quite different.

"This is Tom, and you must teach him to be good," said Mrs. Bedonebyasyoudid, severely.

"I'll try," said the teacher. She did not sound hopeful.

Tom was staring at her with eyes round with surprise. For she was a little girl, no older than himself, with long golden hair that floated around her shoulders like a cloud. She had such a beautiful face that she made him feel like a monster.

The old lady went away. The little girl looked at Tom and thought him very ugly. Tom knew what she was thinking. He thought, "She'll go away, and I shall have no one to help me." Two big tears came into his eyes, and rolled slowly down his prickly cheeks—there wasn't anything he could do about it.

But when the little girl saw those tears, she was suddenly full of pity. She sat down on a rock and he sat beside her, not too close. Then they did their first lesson together.

After that, she came every day except Sundays. The lessons weren't like the ones in schools on land. They were never difficult or boring. The only thing Tom found hard was to do without her on Sundays.

Little by little, his horrid spines disappeared—until the morning came when they had all gone, and he had his smooth, clean skin back again.

Then the little girl looked at him and exclaimed, "But I know who you are! You're the chimney sweep who came into my bedroom and gave me such a fright!"

"And you're the little girl I saw lying there asleep!"

Hooray! They were so pleased to see each other again!

"How did you get here?" asked Tom.

"I went for a walk by the sea, and I slipped and fell, and hit my head on a rock. I was trying to catch a water baby."

"That was you! But it was me!" cried Tom.

"You! In the net?" cried Ellie.

Then they told each other all their adventures. The lesson was often interrupted that day, because they kept remembering more things that had happened and must be told.

So the time passed quickly in talking and teaching and learning. Time passed—days into weeks, weeks into months—but they hardly noticed it, because nothing much changed in their world under the water, and they were so happy together.

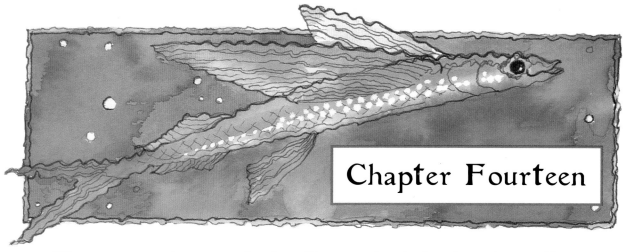

Chapter Fourteen

Ellie came every day except Sundays. Tom wondered a lot about this, and he grew more and more curious to know where she went on that day, and what she did when she was not with him.

"Did you have a good time?" he always asked first thing on Monday morning.

"Very good!"

"Where did you go?"

Her answer was the same every week. "I went home."

"Where is your home, Ellie? I wish you'd tell me about it." But she never could. She only said, "It's a beautiful place."

"What do you mean—beautiful? Is it better than here?"

"Oh yes, of course—much better!"

"I wish I could go there," he said, discontentedly. "I'd like to see it. Why can't I go there with you?"

"I don't know."

"Where is it, anyway?"

"I don't know. I'd tell you if I could. I wish you'd stop going on about it, Tom! Isn't it enough that we have six days of the week together?"

But it wasn't enough for Tom. As time passed, the idea that Ellie had some wonderful place to herself, where he was not allowed to be, began to spoil his happiness. He thought about it constantly and imagined that Ellie didn't like him, not really—because if she did she would take him home with her.

"If I had a beautiful place to go to, I'd want you to see it," he told her one day, resentfully.

"Oh, Tom! It isn't for me to decide. Why don't you ask Mrs. Bedonebyasyoudid, if you want to go there so much?"

So he did. The old lady looked at him gravely through her green spectacles. She said, "No one can go there unless they earn the right."

"What does that mean? I don't understand. Is it something I have to do? Tell me! I'll do it!"

"You sound very confident," she said with a sour smile.

"I'd do anything to go to Ellie's home. I want to see it for myself."

"All right! But it won't be easy. It can't be easy for anyone. You see, if you really want to go to that special place—and it is more wonderful and more beautiful than anything you can imagine—first of all you have to go somewhere where you don't want to go, and do things you don't enjoy doing, and help somebody you really don't like."

"But is that what Ellie did?"

"You'd better ask her!"

Then Ellie looked very embarrassed. "I did, Tom. I didn't want to come here a bit. And you know, I'm sorry, but I didn't like you at all, because. . . ."

"Because I was so prickly. But I'm not now, am I?"

"Of course not! I really like you now, and I love coming here, and our lessons, and everything."

"There you are!" said the old lady triumphantly. "Maybe one day you'll like going where you don't want to go, my dear Tom, and being useful to someone you hate."

So now Tom knew what he had to do, but he didn't want to do it. He pretended to himself that he didn't care any more about going home with Ellie, but it wasn't true.

When she came the next day, he felt awkward and ashamed, because he imagined that she thought him a coward. He got angry with her, because she had done what he couldn't do, and he imagined she felt superior. Ellie couldn't understand what was the matter with him. He was in such a bad temper that she lost heart and went home early. Then Tom was unhappier than ever.

Now that he knew about that beautiful place, and how impossible it was to get to it, he couldn't stop thinking about it. He had no peace, day or night.

At last he burst out, "I'm so miserable, and everything here has turned so stupid, I suppose I shall have to go—only you must come with me, Ellie."

"I can't," she said sadly. "I wish I could, and that's the truth, but I know you have to go alone."

"I might have guessed! I can guess what I've got to do, as well—find horrible old Grimes. I certainly hate him. And much chance I've got of helping him—he won't listen to anything I say! Besides, if I do manage to find him, he'll turn me back into a chimney sweep." And he bit his fingernails, and started sniveling. "That's what I've been dreading all along."

"No, no—that's impossible! No one can turn you back into a sweep, as long as you are brave and good."

"Brave and good!" repeated Tom in a sneering tone. "Brave and good! That's fine, coming from you! The truth is you don't like me any more, and you're tired of coming here. You're trying to make me go away because you've had enough of it!"

"That's a lie," said Ellie, and her eyes filled with tears. "How can you say that? How can you even think it?" Then suddenly she cried out, "Tom! Where are you?"

"Ellie!" he shouted, desperately. "Oh, Ellie! Come back!"

For they couldn't see each other. He heard her crying, "Tom! Tom!" But her voice grew fainter and fainter—until at last he couldn't hear her at all.

Then he was in a panic. He swam as fast as he could among the rocks, and around the great colored pillars under the island; he searched everywhere, but he couldn't find her. He shouted, but she didn't answer; he asked his friends but no one had seen her. At last, in desperation he floated to the surface and shrieked for Mrs. Bedonebyasyoudid. That was the best thing he could have done, because she came in an instant.

"Oh dear, oh dear!" he cried. "I think I've killed Ellie!"

"Rubbish," said the old lady. "I sent her home, that's all, because you were so nasty to her."

"Bring her back! I'm sorry, I'm sorry!"

"Now, Tom! It's time you grew up and stopped behaving like a baby. You must go out and see the world, and learn for yourself what is good and what is bad, and how to be responsible. If you're so fond of Ellie, you want her to be proud of you, don't you?"

This was a new idea to Tom, and he liked it. But then he remembered what he had to do, and his spirits fell.

"I suppose you mean I have to go and find Mr. Grimes," he said, gloomily. "I don't know where he is, and I certainly don't want to see him again."

"Mr. Grimes is at the Other-end-of-Nowhere."

"Where's that?"

"Listen carefully. First, you must go to Shiny Wall, and through the white gate that has never been opened. Then you will find yourself in Peacepool, where whales go when they die. Mother Carey lives in Peacepool. If you still want to go on, you can ask her the way to the Other-end-of-Nowhere."

"Who is this Mother Carey?"

"You will know her as soon as you meet her. She never moves from Peacepool."

"Shiny Wall," said Tom. "Shiny Wall—I don't know how I'll find it."

"You've a tongue in your head, haven't you?" the old lady said sharply. She was getting impatient. Tom touched her timidly on the arm.

"Would you mind if I asked for something? It's going to be such a long journey. Maybe I won't ever come back."

"Don't worry about that!" she said. "Be brave and good, and you will certainly come back safe and sound!"

"Still it won't be for a long time—years and years, probably."

"Oh—very well! What do you want me to do?"

"Do you think . . . would it be possible, before I go, just to say goodbye to Ellie?"

"What do you want to do that for?"

"It would encourage me in the hard times," said Tom in a small voice.

Immediately, there stood Ellie. Tom looked at her. He wanted to remember her face exactly.

"I'm going now, Ellie. It's a long way, and I don't know when I'll be back."

"I wish you weren't going, Tom, but you must. I shall think about you all the time," she said.

"I'm sorry I was angry. I didn't mean it."

"I know. It's all right."

They stood for a little while in silence. The old lady cleared her throat.

"Goodbye then, Ellie!"

"Goodbye. I'll wait for you here. Take care of yourself, dear Tom! Good luck!"

And then, in the blink of an eyelid, the island, and Mrs. Bedonebyasyoudid, and Ellie disappeared. Tom found himself alone in the great, rolling sea.

Chapter Fifteen

Tom was afraid—very afraid. He had no idea where he was, and there was nothing about to ask. It was all he could do not to burst into tears and scream for help—like a baby!

But—"Courage," he told himself. "I can't give up before I've even started." So he started to swim. Where? Anywhere!

After a while he floated to the surface, and rocking on the gray-green water, called out to some gulls that were flying overhead.

"Shiny Wall! Shiny Wall! Never heard of it!" they shrieked. However, one came down in the sea near Tom, who looked sideways at its long, cruel beak, and its beady black eye.

"Shiny Wall," said the big white-and-gray bird, thoughtfully. "That sounds like ice. Perhaps you should head north?"

"Thank you very much," said Tom.

"Remember, it's cold up there! You'd better grow some feathers!"

The other gulls were circling above them, and screamed with mocking laughter when they heard this solemn advice. Then they all flew away, but Tom squinted up at the sun and struck out northward with a brave heart.

He had been swimming for several hours when he saw a huge ship on the horizon. He was afraid she was on fire at first, for she carried no sails and trailed a long cloud of smoke. Then he remembered hearing some of the water babies discussing such things—steamships, they called them—and he swam closer to have a look. Some dolphins were playing in her foaming wake, and he joined them and had a lot of fun leaping and diving and somersaulting, before he thought of asking them the way; but they were such jolly, carefree creatures, they never learned anything if they could help it, and though they liked the sound of a Shiny Wall, they couldn't tell him about it.

It was disappointing. When he was tired of playing, Tom floated near the great hull, watching the passengers strolling about on deck. At last a beautiful woman came out and stood just above him against the rail. She was dressed all in black, for she was a widow, and had a baby in her arms. She sang to the baby, while it laughed at the waves—it was a sad little song that she sang. Then the baby saw Tom, and stretched out its arms, and began struggling as if it wanted to join him in the water.

"What's the matter, my darling? What are you looking at?" The lady stared down at the sea, and then she, too, caught sight of Tom where he swam in the foam below the ship.

She cried out with surprise, and then he heard her say quietly, "Why not? Why shouldn't there be babies in the sea?" She waved and smiled at Tom, and blew him a kiss.

He ducked and turned somersaults to amuse the baby. But presently an old woman, also dressed in black, came out and put her arm around the lady's shoulders and led her away. So he let the ship pass, and then he turned again to the north; but he looked back often. He saw her lights come on, one by one, as the sky darkened. Little by little, she slid away, and her smoke was lost in the evening mist.

Tom traveled north for several days, holding a steady course according to the stars by night and the sun by day. All the time the water was getting colder, but that didn't matter to his water-baby body. When he felt lonely or frightened in that wide, cold, gray sea, he thought about Ellie. Her face was like a light in his mind that gave him courage.

At last he chanced to meet the King of the Herrings perched on a little throne made of seaweed, gobbling sprats. He looked up at Tom with one sticking out of his mouth, like a cigar, and he tossed it up and caught it, like a dog with a sugar lump, before speaking with his mouth full.

"What are you doing up here, young fellermelad? You're a long way from home!"

"Excuse me, Sire, but could you please tell me how to get to Shiny Wall?"

"Shiny Wall! There's only one person who could tell you that—the old bird who sits on the Allalonestone. She does nothing all day but remember. She may remember how to get to Shiny Wall."

Then the King explained the way to the Allalonestone, which was a solitary rock and easily missed.

So Tom thanked him and swam on. But as luck would have it, a flock of petrels passed by, twittering and darting over the waves like swallows. He called out to them.

"Shiny Wall? Come with us, we'll take you part of the way! We are Mother Carey's chickens—didn't you know that? She sends us out to guide good birds home."

So Tom joined the petrels. They turned northeast, and as they went, the sea got rougher, and the wind began to blow hard. But luckily the storm was behind them, so they went on at high speed, and once Tom got used to it, he grinned with excitement as he skimmed the waves with the petrels.

But then they came on a dreadful thing—a huge ship lying on her side. Her deck was swept clean by the waves; her funnel lay wallowing in the water, with a surging tangle of ropes and spars. The petrels flew over her, mourning; but Tom managed to scramble onto the heaving wreck and stared about him in grief and terror. Then he noticed a baby's cot, firmly tied under the bulwark, and in it lay a child, fast asleep. It was the one he had last seen laughing in its mother's arms.

He struggled toward it, but a small black-and-brown terrier jumped out, and barked and snapped to stop him from getting at the baby. But, ah!—just then, a huge green wave towered over the ship, and collapsed on the three of them. It wrenched the cot free and swept them all into the hungry sea.

"What about the baby?" screamed Tom. Then he saw the water fairies waiting there in the green tide. They took the cot with the sleeping baby in it, and he knew that they would carry it safely in their magical arms all the way to the island that was the water babies' home.

The dog kicked and struggled in the sea, and coughed and spat, until with a tremendous sneeze he turned himself into a water dog. So he dashed at Tom, and licked his legs, and nipped him, and grinned, and barked, and from that moment took part in all his adventures.

The petrels flew on, and Tom and the dog followed. At last they saw a mountain peak high above the clouds, which sparkled as if it was made of sugar. Nearby there was a flock of large birds, picking the bones of a dead whale.

The petrels gathered around Tom. "One of those fellows will take you the rest of the way," they said. "We daren't fly over the ice, but they are so big and bold, they don't care what they do."

The dog barked, and Tom looked askance at the scavenging birds. But they were kind, in a rough way, when they understood what he wanted.

"Shiny Wall, is it? Easy job!" shouted their leader. "I'll carry you on my back, and you, John, you take the dog." The terrier was seized by the scruff, and the whole flock rose into the air, cracking jokes and hooting with laughter. "Lord, Lord, what little 'uns you are! You wouldn't have been much use to us where we come from!"

"Where's that?" shouted Tom above the racket of the flight.

"We are the spirits of the hunters who went after whales, through perilous seas and rough weather. Never fear! We'll land you safe at Shiny Wall!"

Now they were flying low over the ice pack, and the huge blocks of ice ground together, and heaved and groaned in the swell. Tom could see the wrecks of many gallant ships trapped in the ice, some with sails still up, frozen white and stiff, and the rigging like cobwebs on a frosty morning.

But at last they were safely over, and there was Shiny Wall, glimmering through the snowstorm. Tom and the dog were put down gently at the foot of it.

"Where's the gate?" shouted Tom above the blizzard, while the dog shook the snow out of his fur.

"What gate? There isn't one!" shrieked the birds.

"Then how can I get through the Wall?"

"You can't, and you can't climb over it, that's for sure! You'll have to dive under it! Good luck!" Then the brave birds flew away in a cloud, calling, "Good luck! Good luck!" till their cries vanished in the distance.

There were cracks in the ice where the water must be. Tom peered in. It looked black and dreadful. But he hadn't come so far to turn back now! He patted the dog, took a deep breath, and dived.

Down, down, down. Now there was no light left. He went right down
to the bottom of the sea, and he swam in complete darkness for a week.
He was glad of his companion then. The dog never whined or complained, but
paddled along steadily beside him. At last he saw a faint radiance ahead. His
heartbeat quickened.

Sure enough, the water was getting light! He had passed under Shiny Wall.

Chapter Sixteen

The water became light and clear—as clear as crystal. As Tom floated up, clouds of sea moths fluttered around his head, all colors of the rainbow. The terrier wriggled with joy and snapped at them, and at the shrimps and jellyfish nearer the surface. And at last they looked out and saw that they were in Peacepool.

It was more of a sea than a pool, surrounded by cliffs of ice in all kinds of shapes—obelisks and spires, pyramids, towers, and battlements. Here the sun never set, but circled the ice, just peeping over it, and sparkling on it in waves of marvelous color, blues and pinks and yellows and greens. It threw shining bridges across the caves where the ice fairies lived, and flashed reflected rays and fiery arcs through the sky. The air was so clear that the farthest cliffs could be seen in every detail, and it was so quiet that one could hear a whale blink. These huge beasts looked like the hulls of ships in harbor, as they lay warming their backs on the surface, and when they breathed out a water spout, the sun turned it into a rainbow.

It was such a beautiful place, it made Tom happy just to look at it. But then he remembered how far he still had to go, and he swam toward the whale lying nearest to him. Usually he would have felt timid about talking to such a gigantic beast, but everything there was so calm that he felt perfectly safe. The whale opened one eye and watched him approach.

"Please, how shall I find Mother Carey?"

"That's her, in the middle."

"What do you mean—that iceberg?" cried Tom in amazement.

"It's no iceberg. Go and see for yourself! You can take all the time in the world—she never moves. She can't. She's too busy."

"What does she do?"

"Do? Why she makes new beasts out of old, day in, day out, year in, year out. What sort of place have you come from that you don't know that?"

All this time the terrier had been gamboling around the great whale with little sharp barks that echoed around the mountains. Tom called him to heel, and swam toward the great, solitary, sparkling white block in the center of the pool. As he approached, he saw that the iceberg was indeed a lady of gigantic size, seated on a pure white throne and entirely white herself except for her blue, blue eyes, which gazed kindly down upon him. She did not look busy. She was resting her large chin on her huge hand, and her huge elbow on her enormous knee. She was old—as old as the world itself, for her hair, which had never been cut, almost covered her with glittering whiteness.

"What can I do for you, my little fellow? I haven't seen a water baby here for I don't know how long."

"Please," said Tom, "I want to go to the Other-end-of-Nowhere. Could you tell me the way?"

"But you already know it."

"Do I? Then I've completely forgotten it."

"Look at me."

So he looked up into her blue eyes, and then he remembered exactly how to get to the Other-end-of-Nowhere.

"Of course, I do know," he said. "I'm sorry to have troubled you. The whale told me how busy you are."

"That's true."

"Are you making new beasts out of old?"

"That's right."

But how could she do that, sitting there all the time without moving so much as a finger? She wasn't even holding a pair of scissors, or a needle and thread!

"I'll let you into the secret of it," she said, as if she could read his thoughts. "I think into them, and make them make themselves."

It was true, but more than Tom could understand.

"Now tell me," she went on. "Are you quite sure of the way to the Other-end-of-Nowhere?"

Alas! Tom had completely forgotten it.

"That's because you aren't looking at me," Mother Carey said with a smile.

So he looked at her again, and then he remembered. But as soon as he looked away, he forgot.

"Oh dear!" he exclaimed. "How shall I ever find it? I can't keep looking at you if you're here, and I'm somewhere else!"

"Cheer up, it's quite simple," she said kindly. "You must follow your dog. He knows how to get there by instinct. But remember, the dog will walk behind you, so you will have to travel backward."

"Backward!" cried Tom. "How shall I see where I'm going?"

"You won't, but believe me, it is the only way. If you look in front of you, you won't be able to see anything at all. You must go backward, and keep your eyes on the dog. Then you'll discover what is ahead of you as clearly as if you were the right way around."

Tom was astonished, and a little dismayed to hear this, but he didn't argue about it. It was not possible to doubt Mother Carey.

"Now," she said, "I am going to give you a special passport, which you must keep safely at all times." Then she produced a sheet of parchment folded small and attached to a string, which he fastened carefully around his neck. "You are sure to meet some very peculiar people," she went on. "They may try to stop you, but when they see this, they will have to let you through. There is nothing more I can do for you, my dear, but give you my blessing, and remind you to follow my instructions, which will bring you safely to your journey's end. So go on bravely and carefully, and keep your eyes on your dog."

All this time the terrier had been sitting quietly at Mother Carey's feet, so that Tom was surprised and pleased to see that he did know how to behave. But when the great lady said this, he yapped once and, getting on his hind legs, reached up to lick her hand. Tom thanked her gratefully. Then he said goodbye and called his dog to toe, because he had to travel backward. After a long swim (backstroke), and a steep and difficult climb back to front through the ice mountains, they left Peacepool for ever.

Chapter Seventeen

No sooner had Tom landed safely on the other side of the ice mountains, than all sorts of weird, oddly-dressed people came hurrying up. They were magicians and conjurors, people who said they could tell the future from stars or tea leaves or a crystal ball, prophets and forecasters of every kind. They crowded around him, shouting, "Which way do you think you're going? Turn around, turn around! We'll show you what's going to happen to the world!"

Tom thought he had better show them his passport, but it only made them angry. "What sort of old-fashioned rubbish is that?" they demanded. "How can you ever do anything in the world if you don't get up to date? This is what you ought to be looking at!" And they pushed forward to try to turn him around by force. But the terrier growled and snarled so ferociously, and Tom kept on his way (backward) so steadfastly, that they had to give up, and their shouts faded away in the distance.

By and by, the travelers reached the brink of a pale ocean the color of skimmed milk. They slipped into it and went down, down, until they could walk along the bottom. It was ghostly there. There were no rocks, or weeds, or any living thing. The ground they walked on was white and soft, like ashes, and Tom kept looking at the dog, and the dog looked ahead through the twilight.

After a while, Tom became aware of a throbbing sound in the distance, which turned into hissings, and roarings, and thumpings as they approached, as if all the steam engines that had ever been invented were working away at once. Soon the water began to get hot, which luckily didn't matter at all to him or his dog; but as it got hotter, it thickened till it was like thin porridge, and it had a nasty smell. Now Tom kept stumbling over the shells and bones of fish that had died there, and the engine noise was deafening.

At last the little dog sat down and whined, and Tom saw that there was a board put up, like a place-name, with one word written on it—STOP. So he

did. He was on the rim of a hole, like a well to the center of the earth. This was where the noise was coming from, and clouds of steam were gushing out of it, making a white jet all the way up to the surface of the dirty sea. But when he tried to peer into the deep, deep pit, wondering what could be down there to make all that noise and steam, a handful of pebbles shot up and hit him hard in the face. For the steam sucked away at the rim of the hole, the way a wave sucks at the seashore. It hurled it up into the water and then drew it back again in a deluge of mud and gravel. It was a fearful, furious place, and just as Tom was wondering how the dog would manage to get them across, the ground where he stood was ripped off and blasted upward, and away he whirled with the dog, hurtling toward the surface! They would have traveled goodness knows how many miles like rockets if there hadn't been something in the way.

Crash! They were breathless and giddy, but neither was hurt. Tom was jammed in the legs of the most fantastic, living engine he could possibly have imagined.

It was hovering over the steam on half a dozen wings, arranged in a circle like the sails of a windmill. From each wing hung down a leg, with a claw like a comb at the end, and it had one eye in its middle, and a mouth all on one side like a flatfish. It screeched at Tom, and tried to shake him off, but he only gripped it more tightly.

"I'm sorry!" he shouted at the thing.

"I'm on a journey to the Other-end-of-Nowhere! I won't stop long!"

"Yah!" shrieked the engine. "Don't give me that! You're after my gold, and don't you deny it!"

Then Tom saw what the engine was doing. As the steam gushed up, it cleaned it with its combs, and as it billowed against its wings, the vapor was changed into metal. Gold dust dropped from one wing, silver from another, copper, tin, lead, and platinum all fell from different wings. These dusts fell back into the deep mud below, to find their way eventually into the rocks of the world.

Suddenly, without any warning, the steam shut off. The deep, deep hole was empty for an instant, like a tube into the earth's heart, and then seawater poured into the vacuum, so fast that the poor old engine whizzed around like a top. Tom just heard it screeching, "If you're really on a journey, now's your chance to jump off! Yah! I don't believe it!"

"Thanks!" yelled Tom, and he jumped and shot down the cataract like a leaf in a waterfall, and the dog shot with him.

So they got to the bottom safely, and the dog swam, and Tom swam backstroke, till they reached the farther shore of that wide, pale, deadly sea, and now they were in the Other-end-of-Nowhere.

Chapter Eighteen

Tom walked, and the dog walked, and at last they came to a town. They could hear it long before they reached it because it was so noisy. In that place, everybody meddled in everyone else's business, and thought they knew better than anyone else; but it was an ugly, dirty city, where they didn't even empty the dustbins, because everyone thought somebody else should do it.

As soon as Tom and his dog walked into the main square, all the inhabitants stopped what they were doing and rushed up to show him the way, without bothering to ask him which way he wanted to go.

"Go west, go west, young man!" cried one, who was wearing a cowboy hat.

"No, no—he wants to go north. This is the way to the north! Follow your nose and you can't go wrong!" said a fellow wearing a kilt and carrying some broken bagpipes.

"The east—home of meditation, tranquillity, and repose—is this way, I assure you," said a solemn man with a mouth like a rabbit.

"He wants to go south! He wants me to explain to him how to go to the south!" cried another, pushing forward and brandishing a medieval atlas.

"Thank you, but I know where I'm going," said Tom, out of breath, as they shoved him and poked him and pulled him in all directions.

"Oh no, you don't!" they all shouted together. "Don't you believe it! Whichever way you are going, you are going wrong!"

Tom was surrounded by a shouting, gesticulating mob, who were much too excited to read his passport, and he was afraid they would tear him in pieces in their anxiety to put him on the right road. The dog was afraid for him, too. He suddenly lost his temper and dashed at the townsfolk, biting them so severely on the legs and ankles that they soon fell back, and the travelers were able to escape.

They left that land and came to another, which was a pretty place and might have been nice to live in. But the inhabitants spent all their time running away, they didn't know why. All they did was run with their hands over their ears, screaming, "Don't tell us about it! Oh, don't tell us! We don't want to hear about it! We can't bear it!"

Tom stood and watched as a crowd dashed past him. In front was a man trying to shear a pig, which cantered along like a pony and squealed all the time. If the panic-stricken islanders had any comfort, it was the thought of wearing pig's wool one day.

But at the back ran a poor old giant, so shabby and thin that Tom felt sorry for him at once. He was as flimsy as if he was made of wire and paper stuck together with glue. He wore huge, thick spectacles cracked in several places that bounced on his bony old nose, and carried a butterfly net in one hand and a hammer in the other. He was hung all over with scientific equipment, such as specimen boxes, cameras, microscopes, preserving bottles, scalpels, tweezers, and so on. These flopped about on his poor bent body, and to make matters worse, he was running backward, without any dog to guide him, and going as hard as he could.

Tom did not move out of the way, so the giant saw him standing there as soon as he passed. He stopped at once and cried out, in a high, weedy voice, "Well done! Who are you, my little fellow? Why aren't you running away?"

"I am Tom, and I am a water baby, and this is my dog."

"Water baby, water baby," repeated the giant excitedly, feeling around himself with one hand for a bottle to catch Tom in while he took off his spectacles with the other in order to see him better. But Tom dodged behind him out of sight.

"Oh no, you don't!" he said. "I've swum across the world, and dived under the world, and met Mother Carey, and got as far as this—and I don't mean to be caught by you, thank you very much!"

The giant was so astonished by this speech that he dropped his bottle and sat down by Tom. He asked many questions about his journey, and peered at his passport from Mother Carey, reading the words aloud in a wondering tone.

"Oh, you lucky little chap!" he exclaimed at last. "Don't I wish I'd done all that!"

"Why don't you turn yourself into a water baby? It's quite simple; I can tell you what to do."

"I can't! How can I ever be a child again? It's impossible," said the giant, and two huge tears sploshed from his eyes onto the dog, who had to get up and shake himself.

"Don't you think you're wasting your time running after all those silly people?" asked Tom, when his friend was cheerful again.

"No, no, my dear—you've got it all wrong! *They* are running after *me*! They call me names, and throw stones, and tell me what they'll do to me when they catch me; but they never will, you see, because I just grow bigger, and run faster the farther I go. Believe me, I only want to be friends with them. I only want to tell them certain important facts it would be to their advantage to know. But I can't get them to listen!"

"Why not stop and let them catch you? You could sort it out then."

"My dear little chap, if I stopped, think of all the grubs and maggots and flies and mosses I wouldn't be able to discover! And then, if I stopped discovering things, I'd die—I'm sure of that. In fact, now that I think of it, while I've been sitting here chatting to you, I must have missed a dozen new species!"

So up he scrambled with his old joints snapping, and on he galloped; and on went Tom with his dog in the opposite direction, feeling very sorry for his deluded friend.

When they came to the next land, Tom heard a gloomy noise—a moaning and groaning, whining and howling, crying and grumbling that made him wonder what in the world could be happening. He had not gone very far before the dog gave a growl, and he saw a large notice. It simply said, NO TOYS.

This was a shock, and at the same time he began to make sense of the noise. It was the song of the Tomtoddies (all heads and no bodies). It was the only song they knew, and they sang it day and night. It had just one line. "I can't learn my lesson—the examiner's coming!"

The dog joined mournfully in this chorus.

Tom looked around for the unfortunate children who were singing it. There weren't any; he couldn't see any people here at all. He was surrounded by big bulbous vegetables—beets and turnips, radishes and mangel-wurzels, lying on the hard earth without any green. They one and all began to cry out to him, "I can't learn my lesson—the examiner's coming!"

"Please help me! What is twenty-nine times twenty-nine divided by one-and-a-half?"

"How do you find the square root of a circle?"

"What river is Georgia on—if it is on a river?"

"How many people lived in Baghdad in 1541?"

"But I don't know any of that!" exclaimed Tom. So he couldn't help them, not even a poor weepy turnip that begged him to tell him anything, anything at all of general information.

"I'm afraid I don't know General Information," said Tom. "I don't know much about the army, but I had a friend who was a drummer. I can tell you about him if you like."

So he described the adventures of the boy he had known when he was a chimney sweep, and the turnip listened carefully, but the more he listened, the more he forgot, and the more water he shed.

This was very distressing to Tom. He hurried on until he tripped over an old stick lying on the ground.

"Watch where you're going," growled the stick.

"Sorry! Please, as you live here, can you explain why those poor vegetables over there are trying to learn things when they can't?"

"It's not their fault," growled the stick. "They've been badgered, and pressurized, and crammed, at home and at school, day in, day out, till they've about lost their wits. It's a shame. I hate it."

"I wish I could help them! I wish I could stop their crying," said poor Tom.

"You can't! They aren't crying anyhow. That's the last of their brains, excaping into the fresh air. You can't blame them! I never heard such rubbish as they try to cram in. That examiner—he's a villain, he is! Never mind."

"I wish Mrs. Bedonebyasyoudid could get him!"

"She can," said the stick. "She will! And I tell you what—she's promised me that I shall have the thrashing of him! So I'm waiting for that day. I'm looking forward to it!"

And the gruff old stick settled back in the dust.

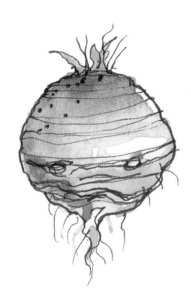

Chapter Nineteen

Now Tom came to a wide and barren plain without any trees or plants at all, where no birds sang or flew in the empty air. It was as forlorn and dusty as a desert, except for one huge building sticking up on the far horizon.

He walked toward it, and very glad he was to have the dog with him, for he had a sinking feeling in his heart that this was where he would find Mr. Grimes. As he approached, he could see that the building was made of bricks and blocks of stone and concrete, reinforced with huge iron girders, with spikes all around the roof. It was tremendously strong, in fact, and tremendously ugly, and if it wasn't a prison, he didn't know what it could be.

Presently some odd-looking things came hopping out, shouting, "Halt in the name of the law!" So he did, and waited with curiosity to see what kind of creatures these could be. He had met such strange things in his travels, he wasn't surprised to find that they were policemen's clubs.

"State your business," snapped the club in front.

"Please, I want to see Mr. Grimes."

"Passport!"

Tom showed his parchment, which was rather crumpled and dirty by this time. The club had one eye in his handle, and had to angle himself very awkwardly to look at it, but he managed to read it without falling over.

"Right, you can pass. I'll go with you," said the club, and his leather thong coiled around his handle, and he hopped along between Tom and his dog, while the other clubs followed at a respectful distance.

"Why do you need a thong when you haven't got a policeman to carry you?" asked Tom.

"To hang myself up by when I am off duty. It would not be in keeping with my position as an officer of the law to lie down in the dirt."

Now they had entered the shadow of the great building. How very dark it was, how grim! There were no windows, only one large iron door with a grating in it. The club hopped forward and struck the door twice with his head.

The grating opened, and Tom looked straight down the mouth of a big brass blunderbuss, ready loaded with shot. He took a hasty step backward.

"What prisoner is this?" demanded the blunderbuss, in a deep voice like the tolling of a bell.

"No prisoner, your honor—just a young lad to see Grimes, the master sweep. He has the correct papers."

"Grimes, Grimes," muttered the blunderbuss, and disappeared to check his lists. "Grimes is in chimney number 345. You'll have to get him up on the roof," he said after a minute, his voice echoing in the dark interior.

Tom stared up, up. The prison wall was at least a mile high, and sheer as glass. However could he climb to the top without any foothold?

"Hold on to your dog," said the club briskly, and Tom took him under his arm. Then the club dashed at him and gave him a shove that whirled him onto the prison roof in an instant.

The roof stretched in all directions, as far as he could see. It was completely flat but for a multitude of brick chimneys, sticking up into the gray sky. He started walking toward them. Soon he was accosted by another club.

"Please, I want to see Mr. Grimes," said Tom.

"All right! Come along, but you won't do any good. I never knew such a fellow. He's the worst of the lot of them. Thinks of nothing but smokes and beer, which we don't allow, and swears the whole time."

As they approached the chimneys, the roof became black with soot and littered with red-hot cinders. But Tom was a water baby. He could walk through the soot without getting dirty, and the cinders couldn't burn him, either. If his heart was beating hard, it was only because he was afraid, very much afraid of meeting Mr. Grimes. The dog gave a yelp, and he realized that he was clutching him harder than was comfortable. So he put him down, and the jolly little animal gamboled about catching hot cinders and tossing them in the air, and trying his best to make his master feel more cheerful.

All the chimneys were marked, and at last they came to the right one. Tom stared at number 345, painted in white on the bricks. He had to force himself to look up. And there he saw his old master, firmly stuck by the shoulders in the top of the sooty chimney under the dreary sky.

Poor Grimes! His bristly hair was full of soot, which ran down his face in streaks whenever it rained and made his eyes water. He had his old pipe stuck in his mouth, but there was no tobacco in it and hadn't been for a long, long time.

"Ahoy there, Mr. Grimes!" shouted the club in a jocular way. "Here's a visitor for you!"

But Grimes only stared ahead of him, and muttered swear words, and something about his pipe, that it wouldn't draw.

"That's enough of that!" snapped the club, and bounced up and knocked him on the head. Grimes struggled to get his hands free to rub the bump, but he couldn't, he was so tightly stuck in the chimney.

Then he did look down. "Well, if it isn't young Tom," he growled. "So you've come to take the mickey! I might have known it."

"No, I haven't," said Tom, who could hardly bear to look at him, he was so changed from the dandy he had known in the old days. "I've come to help you, if I can."

"You get me a bottle of beer, and a packet of smokes and a light. That's all I want."

"I can get you a light, anyhow," said Tom, and he picked up a red hot cinder and climbed the chimney and held it to Grimes's pipe. But it went out at once.

"That's no use," drawled the club, who was taking his ease leaning against the chimney. "You're wasting your time! That man's heart is so cold that it freezes everything near him. You couldn't get his pipe to light, not if you tried for a hundred years."

"That's right, blame it all on me!" shouted Grimes. "As usual! And don't you hit me again! If ever I get my arms free I'll . . . I'll. . . ." He looked wildly around. "I'll get you!"

"Oh no, you won't!" said a familiar voice behind them.

It was Mrs. Bedonebyasyoudid.

As soon as the club saw her, he snapped upright and stood to attention. But as soon as Tom saw her, Mr. Grimes's misery struck him so hard that he buried his face in her skirt and cried.

"There, there!" she said, very kindly. "Don't break your heart! All will be well, believe me."

"What can I do? Can I pull down the chimney?"

"You can try."

So Tom heaved at the bricks with all his strength, but he couldn't shift them.

"It seems such a waste to have come all this way and not be able to help," he said miserably.

"You clear off," said Grimes. "I don't want you blubbering over me. You've a good heart, I don't deny it, but there's nothing you can do. If you hang about here you'll get the hail, which is enough to knock the eyes off your face and that's the truth."

"What hail?" said Tom. The sky seemed calm, though gray.

"It starts like a soft rain that would do nobody any harm; but when it gets to me it turns as hard as bullets. I dread it, I don't mind telling you. It's as much as I can stand. I wouldn't stand it, if I could do anything else."

"There won't be any more hail," said Mrs. Bedonebyasyoudid. "You know very well what it was, because I told you. Your mother used to cry for you, every night, when she said her prayers, and it was your cold heart that froze those tears to hailstones. But now she is dead, and happy, in Heaven. She won't cry for you any more."

Grimes said nothing for a little while. Then he spoke in a low voice. "So she's dead, is she—my poor old mother. She was a good soul. Yes, she'll be happy in Heaven, and she'd have been happy, too, in that little school she kept in Vendale, if it hadn't been for me."

"Was it her at the school in Vendale?" cried Tom. Then he told Grimes how kind she'd been, even though she couldn't bear chimney sweeps.

"She had good reason to hate them, when I went off and joined them and she never heard from me, nor got so much as a penny from me to help her out in her old age!" And then poor Grimes was racked with sobs, and howled, and tears gushed out of his eyes, and his pipe tumbled from his mouth onto the roof, and broke in pieces.

"Oh, if I could have my life again, what a different man I would be! But it's too late—too late!"

"It is not too late," said Mrs. Bedonebyasyoudid.

And Tom stared. For Grimes's tears were doing what no other tears could do—not his mother's, nor Tom's, nor anyone else's. As they streamed down his face, they washed it clean, and then they washed his shirt front, and then